Book Two

TEARS OF ITALY
(Lacrime d'Italia)

MAZ CALADINE

This book is a work of fiction. The names, characters and incidents portrayed in it are the work of the author's imagination. Any resemblance to actual persons living or dead, events or localities is entirely coincidental

Copyright © 2024 Maz Caladine

In Loving Memory of
My Sister,
Chris

Acknowledgements

Photograph of a snowy Mount Vesuvious, Nr Monte Faito courtesy of Joanne Haslam

CONTENTS

The Story So Far	9
Tears of Italy	16
Brother Emmanuel	38
Villa Restoration	45
Monte Faito	53
Coronavirus	67
Covid Lockdown	83
Lockdown Anxiety	93
Grand Hotel Italia	101
Wine Cellar	111
Gone Fishing	120
Seeking Comfort	126
Lorenzo	131
John's Secret	136
Lockdown Ends	145
Martha's Confession	151
Homecoming	163
Samantha's News	186
Brother Emmanuel's Fear	192
Boat Trip to Capri	205
A New Life	217
Settling In	232
Grape Harvest	242
Mary's Heartbreak	249
Coronavirus Returns	255
Brother Emmanuel's Death	265
Martha's Plan	274
Surprise Wedding	285
Henrik's Plan	298
The Heat Is On	308
Christmas Day	317
Final Touches	326
Wedding Day	334

THE STORY SO FAR

(Book One – Ti Amo Sorrento)

Main Players

The Villa is a dilapidated old family home tucked away up a long tree-lined drive overlooking the stunning Bay of Naples and Sorrento. Martha, the owner, has turned her traditional home into a thriving restaurant with the help of four English people she met by chance.

Martha Addington - (aged 85) Italian born and brought up in Sorrento by her loving family. She left Italy to marry her late husband, George, a well-respected surgeon. They spent sixty happy years together living in Kensington, London. After his death, she returns to Sorrento to live her remaining years in her family's villa. Martha loves life and people. She encourages everyone with her plans for the restaurant's success. 2019 ends on a high note, and there is much to look forward to in 2020, including plans to expand The Villa into a wedding venue.

Mary Smith – (aged 41) Mary has always relied on herself to cope with life. Her mother abandoned her when she was only hours old, but her confident personality has strengthened her. Martha invites her to work in The Villa; she quits her job as cabin crew for British Airways and puts all her effort into making The Villa a success. Twenty years previously, she had lived in Sorrento and had fallen in love with a young man called Franco. He had been constantly in her thoughts. She has returned to Italy to find him and hopefully rekindle their relationship.

Eva Johnson – (aged 23) is a single English girl who recently qualified from catering college with honours. After her mother's death, she makes an impulsive decision to travel to Sorrento in search of her biological father, Francesco Pascali, a fisherman from Marina Grande, Sorrento. Eva meets Martha, who offers her a job as head chef in The Villa. In 2019, she finds her father, who is delighted to know he has a daughter. They begin to bond and develop a father/daughter relationship. Everything is going well until Eva discovers that Franco is the person Mary has also returned to Sorrento to find.

Giovanni (a stalker) viciously attacks Mary and this results in Mary and Franco being reunited. 2019 ends with Mary and Franco's wedding much to the delight of Eva.

Samantha Marriott - (aged 34) is a nurse from England. Her husband, Robbie, has died of cancer. Her purpose in visiting Italy was to scatter Robbie's ashes in Sorrento, where they were married. She is at a crossroads in her life. After meeting Martha, she eagerly accepts the offer of being involved in The Villa's rebirth, hoping it would give her a new direction but also to remain close to Robbie, whose ashes she scattered on the sea in The Villa's private cove. Everyone tries to help her move on with her life, but she finds it hard. When Mary is in hospital in Naples, Sam meets Dr Lorenzo Rossi (Mary's Doctor). They form a platonic relationship, and Lorenzo offers her a part-time job in the small hospital in Sorrento during the winter. Hard work helps her to put her life back on track.

John Evans – (aged 43) is an ex-army captain. He has a failing leather design business in London. After a disastrous business meeting in Naples, John meets Martha, who invites him to help renovate The Villa and becomes the restaurant manager. He jumps at the chance of a new life. John is a complicated man. He is divorced and suffers moments of OCD (obsessive-compulsive disorder) and PTSD (post-traumatic stress disorder) after his long service in the Army and his time in Afghanistan. John loves his new life. Although he still has moments where his mental health troubles him. He finds affection from Alfie, a lost spaniel, who he rescues and looks after. John is passionate about resurrecting the old vineyard and producing an excellent vintage wine for The Villa.

Henrik – (aged 25) Martha advertises for a sous chef to help Eva run the restaurant, and Henrik is employed. He is from Copenhagen in Denmark, and immediately, the two of them create a good working relationship, resulting in The Villa's success, which exceeds all expectations. Henrik is easygoing and fun to be around. He brings into Eva's life a friendship that is getting stronger every day.

Giovanni – (aged 17) His background is from the streets of Naples. His abusive father had mentally damaged him, and Giovanni had subsequently caused his father's death by drowning. This resulted in him running away and taking refuge in the monastery where the monks had tried to help him. When he noticed people living in The Villa, he began stalking them, taking a particular interest in Mary, and attacked her, leaving her for dead. In his deranged mind, he took his own life by jumping off a cliff when confronted by John. The monks agreed to bury him in their graveyard.

The Monastery and Brother Emmanuel: Situated close to The Villa is an austere Benedictine monastery. It is the home of Brother Emmanuel. He is an elderly monk; much loved by the local community, and has dedicated his life to God.

Signor Miccio – (aged 68) Is Martha's loyal Maître Di employed in her beautiful Hotel Grande Italia in Sorrento centre. He is a small round man with a twinkle in his eyes and has been the inspiration in the hotel's restaurant for many years. His operatic voice and bubbly personality guarantee guests returned year after year. They are delighted to be serenaded at dinner when he gives impromptu singing performance of Neapolitan love songs to rich elderly female guests. He loves women; he loves life and he loves his job.

***

It has been a very successful 2019, and the year ends with everyone looking forward to a new year. They are unaware that a deadly virus has begun infiltrating the world and will inevitably disrupt all their lives.

TEARS OF ITALY
(Lacrime d'Italia)

Sorrento 2020

MAZ CALADINE

January 2020

Martha gazes out of her bedroom window as she rests in the warm rays of the January sunshine. Her beautiful garden looks devoid of colour. Gone is the infusion of magenta-coloured bougainvillea, which is sleeping, waiting for spring to appear so it can once again coil itself around the stone columns and unfurl its blossom to dazzle the world. Her tired eyes focus on the clear blue sea as a sailing boat glides gently by. Its white sails fly freely in the breeze. In the distance, Sorrento glistens in the hazy sunlight. Martha is alone, and the warm air is making her sleepy.

Her mind reflects on the previous year. It had been the right decision to return to Italy after the death of her husband. George is always in her thoughts. It had been a true love marriage. How lucky she was to have met him. He would be so proud of how she had made a new start, especially at 85. She had no regrets about selling their London home and returning to her family's villa. Even the dilapidated state of the house had not fazed her. She smiles as she thinks George had 'arranged' for the four young people to come into her life just when she needed help. They each have their problems, but when she offered them the chance to work for her and turn her villa into a thriving restaurant, they did not hesitate. The Villa, her fabulous home, has now been restored with exquisite taste.

A cloud covers the sun, and her thoughts are turned black and white as she visualises herself as a young girl playing with Alfonso, her dog, in the dusty courtyard. It is not long before her eyes begin to close, and the memories flood in.

***

Sorrento - September 1943

Martha is ten years old and is immersed in

childish pleasures. The sun streams through the tall Cyprus trees, casting playful shadows on the gravel drive. Martha has put out of her mind the horrors of war-torn Italy. She is a child, and poverty and the deprivation that Hitler's Army inflicts on her beloved country have become routine to her. Life before the war started is something she cannot relate to. Her dog is bringing her a rare moment of happiness as he chases a ball and then tantalises her with his refusal to let her have it.

In the distance, she hears the sound of an engine. It becomes louder, and her heart races as she sees the familiar sight of a German BMW R75 motorbike. It zooms up the rough stone drive at high speed and stops before the villa's entrance, sending dust flying into the air and momentarily causing Martha to rub the particles from her eyes.

"Oh no, it's him again." She whispers to Alfonso, who, at the sound of the bike, is almost begging to be picked up.

"Don't worry, sweetie; I won't let him hurt you."

The German soldier clicks his heels and gives a Nazi salute to Martha. She responds defiantly by lifting her chin and glaring at him. Martha doesn't like this man and cannot understand why her father is so friendly towards him. She is relieved when the kitchen door opens, and her Papa, Alberto, comes out to greet him.

"Guten morgen Capitan Hoffman, It is good to see you."

"Signor Russo, Guten morgen. Heil Hitler." He gives a nazi salute, and Alberto reluctantly responds. "I'd like to speak with you now. I am in a hurry."

"Si, please come to my little office where we won't be disturbed."

Martha watches her father lead the way to the wine cellar, where they often talk. She turns away.

"Come on, Alfonso, are you hungry? Let's see what mamma is cooking for lunch."

They head off in the direction of the kitchen, a sorry-looking pair. The hardship of the war is beginning to take its toll on the villagers. Living conditions have become harsh under the German dictatorship, and the bombings from the 'enemy' are constant in the Naples area. Food and clothing are in short supply. The villa needs repair but hasn't been damaged by the bombings.

Valentina and her mother, Rosaria, are busy making pasta in the kitchen. They hardly speak as they effortlessly knead the pasta dough. Both women are lost in their own thoughts.

Upon seeing her granddaughter enter the kitchen, Martha's nonna quickly wipes her flowery hands and stretches out her arms in anticipation of a hug.

"Martha, my darling girl, come here and give me a big kiss," Rosaria reaches out to her. "My word, you are growing so quickly."

Martha dissolves herself into her grandmother's arms. She always feels safe and protected when in her company.

"Look at your feet, girl. It looks like you have been treading grapes. Where are your shoes?"

"Oh, Nonna, I don't like to wear them. They pinch my toes."

"You look like a vagabond, and look at your dress. It's all in tatters."

"Mamma," Valentina interrupted. "We are in the middle of a war."

Rosaria sighs, "I know, but it's hard to see your beautiful granddaughter not wearing a pretty dress. Hopefully, all this will be over soon, and when it is, we shall have a big party with lots of food and new clothes to wear. What do you think of that?" she said as she hugged Martha tightly.

"It will be magical, Nonna. Can I have a dress made of silk with a big bow?"

"Of course, and what colour will you choose?"

Martha thought for a moment. "Ice blue," she replies, "Like in my storybook of the little girl who became an ice skater. She had a lovely dress."

Valentina moved closer to her daughter. "I promise you that is what you will have as soon as these bad times are over." She pinches her cheek and then asks. "Have you seen your father? The food is nearly ready."

"He is with the German man," Martha replied. She was quick to see the anxious look her mother gave her grandmother. Valentina's smile quickly disappeared at the mention of the Capitan. Whenever he was around, she tried to keep out of his way. A few weeks ago, she had been alone in the kitchen. She had become aware of someone standing behind her. It was the Nazi. He swiftly moved forward, grabbing her around the waist tightly, and pushed her hard against the wall. His hand moved to her neck, holding her in place as he roughly moved his other hand over her body. She had remained frozen to the spot, dreading what was to come, but the door opened, and Rosaria stood open-mouthed, staring at the scene in front of her. The Capitan quickly released his grip and laughed loudly as he pushed his way out of the door. Neither woman spoke of the incident, but Rosaria ensured Valentina was never left alone when the German Officer was around.

Valentina said to Martha. "They will have business to discuss. We will eat now, and I'll keep Papa's food warm for him."

They drew their chairs close to the table and huddled over the meagre bowl of pasta. "Here, darling, have some tomatoes. They will fill you up."

"Can I give Alfonso some pasta, mamma?"

"Of course, he can have some of mine. There is no garlic in it, so he should be ok."

"And mine," Rosaria added.

"Mangiare, mangiare (eat, eat)," Martha said to Alfonso as she placed a bowl of food on the floor. He didn't need telling; already, he had started eating as fast as he could. Glancing around the table, a big smile spread over Martha's face. She was happy. If her little dog was fed, then all was well with the world. She didn't even notice there was no meaty sauce or cheese, just some lemon juice and oil to add flavour.

Life had certainly changed for the villagers. From lovingly tending to the rich agricultural land, overnight, they had been forced to allow the German soldiers to steal and eat their crops and stand back as Hitler's Army invaded their world and made camp in their homes.

Martha was used to seeing the German troops in the villages and towns. Nevertheless, the tension and fear in the country increased every day. They soon learnt that a dull sense of acceptance was the only way to cope with life under German control. Recently, she confided her fears in her mother. Valentina was troubled. How can you explain to a young child what happens to your beloved country when war breaks out?

"Martha, we are in the midst of a world war. Our leader, Mussolini, committed Italy to the Germans' side to fight against our enemies. Sometimes, as ordinary people, we don't have a say in how we want our country to be. I don't want you to worry. I know these are not normal times, but they will return, and life will be happy again."

"But why is Papa so friendly with the German soldier? He is a horrible man."

"He is protecting his family, darling. We have always told you to stand up for your true beliefs. Sadly, in a war situation, we are not free to speak, as we would like. Your father may appear friendly with the German Officer, but he doesn't like him or what he represents. In his heart, he knows he has no choice, so we must respect his decision and keep a low profile when the German soldiers are here. Can you do that, mia cara?

"I will try, mamma."

"Good girl," Valentina had said as she hugged her precious daughter tightly. She desperately wanted to cry, but she knew, for the sake of her child, she must keep up the pretence that everything was normal, but with every beat of her heart, she was terrified of what the future held for her family.

After eating her meagre lunch, Martha asked if she might be excused.

"Yes, of course Go outside and play. Nonna and I are baking bread this afternoon."

"Yes, mamma, I will do that."

***

With shaking hands, Alberto unlocks the door to the wine cellar. He tries to remain calm, but it is all an act, just like everything these days. It is important not to let anyone know your true feelings, especially the man behind him. One wrong word and death for him and his family would be instantaneous.

He always has a sense of foreboding when the German Officer turns up unexpectedly. Being a proud Italian, the situation Alberto finds himself and his country in is intolerable. For many years, he has farmed the land with his father. The terrain is rugged, but they produced a good grape and olive crop after much hard work. The fruit trees gave an excellent yield and sold a lot of produce at the local market.

Mussolini, Italy's Fascist leader had invested a lot of money in the terracing of the countryside to help farmers thrive. Then, the emergence of Adolf Hitler and his alliance with Mussolini devastated the country.

The ordinary working people were caught up in a fierce war that Hitler was determined to win.

Any kind of peace and freedom to enjoy the simple things in life had been snatched away from them. Food was in very short supply. Far too many soldiers to feed, and then the bombings started. It was inconceivable to Alberto that anyone would want to destroy not just the towns and villages but the ancient cities full of art and history in his beautiful Italy. And now he finds himself trapped in a situation he cannot escape. He had been forced to allow his home to hide priceless works of art stolen by the Nazis. He was disgusted with himself, but there was nothing he could do except watch as the German soldiers arrived in the middle of the night and forced their way onto his property, unloading magnificent paintings and artefacts of great value in his cellar until it was time to ship them to Austria.

"Quickly, Signor, I have very little time. We have our orders to push north to Anzio. The fighting in Salerno has gone well for our troops." Hoffman moved closer. "We are leaving immediately. I need to talk about the sword. I will not be able to have it transported like the other items. You will have to hide it until I can reclaim it." Alberto listened carefully. There were many rumours the German Army had lost control of Sicily and that the British and Americans had landed in Salerno. He had heard the fighting had been intense and many lives had been lost. The Germans were on the run. He didn't know how he felt about this. He hated Mussolini and Hitler. But the British and the Americans were bombing and destroying his country. Would they be his saviours and liberate his family from this frightening nightmare? He didn't know, and he was terrified.

"Now listen to me. You must find a good hiding place for the sword. The enemy mustn't get their hands on it. Mein Fuhrer wants it for his private collection."

"But I thought the enemy was losing. Surely they are not about to invade Italy?"

The Capitan defiantly replied. "Of course not. There is, however, a strong possibility that the Mafia is being encouraged by the Americans to disrupt the German defences of this wonderful country. As a result, they may make resurgence in this area. Look, Alberto, I am ordering you to take this seriously and not to disobey me."

"What do you mean disobey? We are friends, are we not?"

Hoffman smiled. He was a handsome man, which made Alberto feel anxious. It wasn't easy to judge whether he was genuine or not. Behind his charisma and charm hid a deadly side to his character, and Alberto, many times, had instinctively felt it unwise to cross him.

"Of course, we are good friends, and after this war ends, you must bring your beautiful wife and family to my house in the mountains in Germany as my guest. Now, time is running out. Have you any ideas for a hiding place?"

Alberto glanced around. He was feeling particularly edgy. The main cellar was filled with barrels of wine and racks of bottles. His small room had only a desk and chair. He thought quickly.

"It may be possible to conceal the sword in a false wall. I will wrap it carefully to protect it. I can quickly build a stone frontage in this area."

"Excellent, Signor. I have to leave now. But, remember, I will be back to collect the sword when the war ends. You do understand, don't you?"

Alberto could tell by the tone of the Capitan's voice that this was a threat, and he and his family would suffer if he disposed of the valuable artwork in any way.

"Si, si, I understand. The sword will remain behind this wall until you return. Addio amico mio (goodbye, my friend). I wish you a safe journey."

They shook hands, and the soldier quickly left, leaving Alberto sitting momentarily, taking in all the news. To him, it sounded like the Germans were on the run, and in their place would come the British and the Americans, not to mention the frightening possibility of the Mafia taking over. He had not imagined that things could get more unpleasant, but it looked like they might. To make matters worse, he had a stolen work of art covered in precious diamonds and jewels hidden on his property. Alberto sighed and locked the door to his room. He would build the wall later, but first, he needed lunch and a glass of wine. It was essential to appear normal; otherwise, his wife would get suspicious and worry.

A few minutes later, he was welcomed into the arms of the people he loved most.

"Come and sit down, Alberto. We have saved you some food. Here, have a glass of wine." Rosaria fussed over her son. She turned, smiling at her granddaughter who had followed her father into the kitchen. "Martha, I think Alfonso wants to go outside."

Martha reluctantly took the hint from her nonna. She had been hiding in the wine cellar and had overhead most of the conversation between her father and the German. She wanted to hear what her father had to say but knew it was adult time.

"Has the German Officer gone?" Valentina whispered. She placed a plate of fresh bread and pasta before her husband.

"Yes, my dearest, he has, and apparently, the German army have instructions to move out of the area immediately."

Valentina pulled up a chair. This was good news, indeed.

"So all the rumours are true then. The Germans are losing the war."

"The Capitan said they are regrouping in Anzio, ready for a big push. It's hard to know what to believe. He said the battle at Salerno has gone well for the German Army."

"But if that is the case, why are they pulling out and going north?" Rosaria asked. "It doesn't make sense."

"I agree. He said there was a danger the Americans had made a deal with the Sicilian Mafia to take over the area."

"Do you believe him?" Valentina asked. The prospect of the Mafia being in this area was a terrible shock.

"No, I think the Germans are losing, and that means the liberators will move this way, The

British from the south and the Americans from the north."

"What does that mean for us, Alberto? Will we be safe?"

"I don't know. I really don't know. It is hard to imagine anyone being crueler than the Nazis. We shall have to pray for our family and friends and our country. Now I have some work to do in the wine cellar. I want to take away any trace of the Germans being here."

"Do you need any help?" Valentina asked.

"No, cara, I can manage. You and mamma should walk into the village and warn our neighbours that the Germans are moving out. Take Martha with you. I want to ensure she is always within our sight."

"Yes," Valentina said. "I think we should go and visit the monastery and inform them of what is happening. Also, we can pick up some more food supplies while we can."

Alberto agreed and hugged his mother and then his wife.

"Try not to worry. It may be a good thing if the Germans are losing. Then, hopefully, we will regain our country, and the bombings will stop."

A short while later, Alberto was back in the cellar. He was scared to hold the sacred sword, not knowing where it had been stolen from, but still feeling the reverence of the artwork. It was hewed from a precious metal, possibly gold. He had no idea how old it was, but the value was the priceless jewels embedded into the sword. Even in the dark, the diamonds picked up the light from his candle and sparkled like the night sky. The workmanship of the artwork was exquisite. He knew this was a unique piece, probably very old, and had more than likely been taken from a cathedral or place of importance. Although he was a workingman, he couldn't tell whether a work of art was genuine or forgery. The thought that a significant art piece was in his possession made him feel sick. He surveyed the room. The hiding place had to be perfect; if it were discovered, he would be severely punished if not killed. There was no time to lose. He believed the enemy was advancing. Salerno was only 55 kilometres away. Wrapping the sword in muslin and an old blanket, he carefully laid it against the wall. Fortunately, there was a corner it would fit into. He could build around it with stone from the outside and make it appear as part of the wall. Carefully, he filled the gaps with large rocks, cementing them with a mixture of clay and lime and rubbing dirt over to make his work appear authentic.

'I think this will do. I'm sure nobody would imagine it was a hiding place.' He thought to himself as he cleaned the area where the cement had fallen and then moved his desk in front of the wall. That way, it would be less noticeable. Opening his desk drawer, he took out a bottle of brandy.

The alcohol would calm his nerves. He knew the future was looking uncertain for them all. As he sat back in his chair, he reflected on the Nazi. Thank God this man was going out of their lives. For so long, he had had to pretend he liked him when he really wanted to put a gun into his face and pull the trigger. He would have done it if it hadn't been for his family. No way could he risk their safety. He knew he was right to go along with Hoffman's demands. The fact that he had allowed hundreds of stolen paintings and artefacts to be hidden on his property gave him sleepless nights. So many times in the early hours, he had heard the sounds of the German soldiers loading them onto lorries to be shipped to Germany. How his wife and mother hadn't found out it was a miracle. He knew they realized something was happening but were wise and didn't interfere. Valentina supported him with love and tried to make his worries disappear. He would be forever grateful, and now everything was changing again.

Would the Capitan come back to reclaim his treasure? He couldn't be sure. If the Germans won the war, he would, but if they didn't win, what would he do?

"Leave it hidden in the wall and try and forget about it." He muttered as he took another swig of brandy.

Brother Emmanuel
(Fratello Emanuele)

SORRENTO 2020

The monastery is an imposing building. Its appearance is designed to stop people from peering in through the tiny slits of the windows. It also keeps the monks from looking out at the outside world. The tall stonewalls tower over the hillside and is reached by a long, winding gravel road. Rarely do people travel up to visit. The locals are sensitive to the monks, accepting they live a reclusive life and do not want to be disturbed. Occasionally, villagers see Brother Emmanuel riding his bicycle precariously around the narrow lanes. He is a comical figure, with his long flowing robes trailing in the dirt and perched on his head, at a quirky angle, is his old straw hat. They shout affectionate greetings to him, and he responds by calling out 'Buongiorno Signori.' But that is the total of their involvement. It comforts them to know that the monastery still practices the Catholic faith and that the Brothers are well.

It is a chilly January day in Sorrento. Although the sky is a vivid sapphire blue, Vesuvius, the iconic volcano that dominates the area, has a slight covering of powdery snow on its crater, giving an illusion of smoke cascading down the black volcanic hillside.

Brother Emmanuel is walking slowly to the monastery graveyard. He has risen early, as is his usual routine. It is on his mind to tidy Giovanni's grave. He feels compelled to do so. So often these days, his heart is troubled by Giovanni's brutal death. At night, the old monk tosses and turns in his sleep, and his hard wooden bed with the thin mattress cuts through his bones and wakens him to pain. When he eventually falls asleep, he is tormented by nightmares of himself standing on a cliff edge and a God-like figure pushing him over. He is always grateful to wake up and to know he is in the safety of his own little room.

He looks down at the mound of earth, which is the young man's resting place. It had been a tragic life for the young teenager. If only the

Brothers could have done more to help him. From the moment they had discovered him sleeping rough in one of the greenhouses, they had tried their best to find out where he had come from. But unfortunately, Giovanni was not willing or able to converse with them. It was as though he had taken a vow of silence.

Brother Emmanuel kneels and tenderly pulls out the weeds from the rich earth. He stares at the twisted roots, the tendrils curling around his fingers. His thoughts lead him to his deep-rooted faith in God. So strong is his belief that he has dedicated his life to prayer. But now his loyalty is being tested.

'At least you are at peace now.' The old monk says aloud to the young man buried in the grave. He is still struggling to forgive Giovanni's violent attack on Mary. Long, solitary hours of prayer had confused him about his faith. He had discussed his feelings with the Abbott in detail.

"How can I forgive an act of such brutality?" He had queried. But the Abbott had merely replied that Giovanni was not in his right mind.

"His troubled upbringing has added to his mental state. It is up to us to ask God to forgive him."

Emmanuel pondered for a long time. His prayers reflected his desire to forgive, but his heart struggled.

Thankfully, Mary had recovered, although it was touch and go at the time. Brother Emmanuel's thoughts turned to his meeting with the Signora at The Villa. She had been most welcoming, especially insisting on supplying him with refreshments. He could almost taste the delicious English scones, homemade jam, and cream he was presented with. All his life, his taste buds had been denied such luxuries, and he had suddenly realised the simple pleasure food could bring.

It was a joy to see the villa back to its former glory. It had saddened him to watch how the building had become empty and fallen into disrepair over the years. However, the people now living there were wonderful, and he was impressed with their dedication and hard work in creating a restaurant that was so in keeping with the Italian culture. He smiled to himself. Who would have thought a young English girl would have such knowledge and talent when cooking Italian food.

He sat back on his haunches, and his fingers touched the silver filigree necklace Mary had placed over the simple wooden cross. Tears pricked his eyes. He tried to control them, but deep down, he felt unable to deal with his deep, rooted sadness. Memories from his past kept invading his mind, and no matter how he prayed for guidance, he could not shake off this feeling of utter despair.

Humans were sometimes hard to fathom. Kindness by Mary to someone who had tried to kill her was difficult to understand. He was struggling to get his thoughts in order. He would pray to God tonight for direction. Suddenly, he felt a hand grab his shoulder. He turned, expecting someone to be there. Instead, a chill went through him. He was totally alone.

Fear ripped through him like lightning. He

dragged his weary body away from the grave, and, pulling his hood over his head to keep out the cold wind, he half walked, and half ran back to the safety of the monastery and his room.

Villa Restoration

(Villa Restoration)

John was outside in the courtyard discussing the progress of the vegetable garden with Martha. The ground had been richly manured, and spring vegetables had been planted, ready for the coming holiday season.

"I never realised how the catastrophic eruption of Vesuvius all those years ago would give back to the country such rich and fertile soil," he said to Martha, who instantly agreed.

"It is amazing, John. Nature really does work in strange ways. We are fortunate in this area to be blessed also with warmth. Just look at the lemons from Amalfi. They are so sweet, you can eat them without wincing!"

"Do you think the volcano will ever erupt again?"

"I hope not, but it is active. Thankfully, it is monitored, so there will be adequate warning next time. The last time it erupted was during the war in 1944, as if we didn't have enough to worry about then. I don't think many people died, but if it was to happen again, and the experts think it is due for an eruption, then Naples would be severely at risk."

"My God, it doesn't bear thinking about," John said as a sudden noise made him turn around. "Oh, look, we have a visitor."

They were interrupted by an old Citroen van coming up the driveway.

"I know who this is," Martha said. "It's Enzo, the artist I've been expecting. He's come to give us a quote for painting frescoes on the bedroom walls. Come on, John, I need your artistic eye. Let's see what he can do."

"Buongiorno Signora Addington. My name is Enzo Ricci. I understand you are looking for an artist to do some work for you?"

"Si, Buongiorno Enzo. Thank you for coming. May I introduce you to my restaurant manager, John Evans?"

"Piacere di conoscerti," (so nice to meet you.) John said as he shook Enzo's hand.

"Come inside, and I will explain my ideas to you." Martha had been looking forward to his visit and was keen to hear what he had to say.

Enzo followed her into the elegant reception area.

"What a beautiful place, Signora. I had no idea how magnificent the view is from here. I've lived in Sorrento all my life, and I was amazed when my wife and I came for a meal last year. We were both surprised. I think what you have created is truly special."

"How wonderful, you must come again when we open in March."

"We certainly will. The food was exceptional. Your chef is quite different, and we enjoyed the variety of dishes. Some we had not tried before."

"Ah, Eva is a young English cook. She has a lot of exciting ideas for this year's menus. At the moment, we would like to extend our enterprise into letting rooms. We have permission to conduct wedding ceremonies, and opening some of our bedrooms for guests seems logical. If you want to follow us, I will show you what I have in mind regarding artwork."

Martha opened the door to the first bedroom.

"We have four rooms on this floor, with ensuite bathrooms, and a further four rooms on the third floor. There are two more at the top of the building, but they have been made into one very large suite for the bridal couple. Although the renovations are almost finished, I have been thinking of something to make them more special. This is where your help is needed."

They walked into a spacious, newly decorated room. The large shuttered windows led onto a balcony, which overlooked the courtyard and, in the distance, the town of Sorrento.

"My idea is to give each room a theme," Martha said as she pointed to the facing wall. For example, this might be the Sorrento room. We have had the rooms painted in pastel colours, and I hope you can come up with some ideas. I don't want elaborate paintings. I was thinking of an outline similar to a fresco. It could be Piazza Tasso with silhouettes of people in the main square, not filled in but more impressionistic. What do you think?"

"Are you looking at different scenes in each

room?" Enzo said as he quickly took notes.

"Yes, exactly. There is much scope in this area: Capri, Positano, Amalfi, Vesuvius, Pompeii, Ischia, this villa, and the Bay of Naples. I want simple lines and images, but the bridal suite, perhaps something more colourful, maybe the blue grotto? Is it the kind of work you do? I've heard you are a very talented artist."

"Signora, thank you. I would be more than delighted to submit some designs. I find this project most exciting."

They went through each room, and Enzo took photographs and made some quick sketches as the ideas flowed through his mind.

Martha looked at the young man. He looked like an artist with his short, trimmed beard and long, elegant hands. She was thrilled to hear he was interested in the project. It had always been her passion to nurture and help young emerging talent.

"Signora, I have a few sketches to work with and would be happy to come and see you in a few days. Do you have a start date and a time limit?"

"We will be ready to open the restaurant on the 15th of March, and I believe our first wedding is booked for the middle of June."

"That would fit in nicely with my schedule. If you are happy with my designs, I could start immediately and be ready when you open."

"Thank you, Enzo. I appreciate you coming, and I look forward to seeing your ideas. Have you time for some refreshments, perhaps a coffee?"

"Yes, Signora, that would be very welcome."

"Good, follow me, and I will show you the kitchen where all the hard work is done."

Back down the winding staircase, Enzo glanced up at the massive chandelier.

'You have made The Villa charming. I love how you have created the feeling of the traditional home but with a sense of elegance."

"We have worked hard this last year and have many plans for the future."

"I cannot see how you can fail. Sorrento is a special place. It is perfect for such a classy restaurant."

"Thank you, Enzo. We cannot wait for the season to start again."

Monte Faito

(Monte Faito)

Two weeks later, Martha woke feeling quite cold. She stood looking out of her bedroom window and was delighted to see Vesuvius had a covering of snow. The crater seemed serene, with the whiteness silhouetted against a deep mauve sky.

Eva knocked at the door and entered, carrying a breakfast tray.

"Eva, my dear, come and look at this," Martha said as she pulled back the long drapes.

"Wow! That can't be snow, surely."

"Yes, it often snows in the winter. It looks quite majestic, doesn't it? You and Henrik should take advantage of the weather and head to Monte Faito. You will enjoy it up there. The views are wonderful overlooking Naples, and there will be enough snow to have fun."

"Oh, that sounds amazing. I'll go and see if Henrik wants to go."

"Take the car. It will be difficult on your Vespas.

The cable car is closed in the winter. And remember to take some photographs for your website. It is a perfect opportunity to get out in the fresh air."

"I will, Martha. It sounds like a beautiful idea."

"What is Samantha doing? Maybe she would like to go with you?"

"She's been called into the hospital. Lorenzo rang earlier. He sounded quite distressed about something."

"I hope it's nothing to do with the virus." Martha poured a cup of coffee and settled in her armchair. "I heard on the news last night that two cases have been identified in Lombardy."

"Really, did they say any more about it?"

"They don't know what it is yet. It's all a bit of a mystery. Let's hope it is nothing serious. John said it had come from somewhere in China. But how it's ended up here, they have no idea."

"What are you doing today, Martha? Have you any plans? Would you like to come with us?"

"I would love to, but I'm afraid my old bones would not be very good in snow. John and I are going to have a look at the vineyard we have someone coming to give us some advice. Then at some stage we need to open up the wine cellar. It's been years since I've been down there. We hope to clear it out and turn it into something special."

"Enzo may be able to do some more of his paintings on the wall. Big bunches of grapes would be in keeping for a wine cellar."

"It's worth thinking about. He is doing a wonderful job on the rooms. It has added something special, and he's almost finished the bridal suite. The colours are superb."

"Do you think the kitchen would look good with a scene mimicking the outside terrace?"

"I like that idea. A bit like bringing the outside in. I'll have a word with him." Martha replied.

Eva agreed. "I can't wait to open up. I've missed cooking and all the people."

"It will, cara, but while you have some free time, you get off and enjoy your day."

Back in the kitchen, Henrik jumped at the chance for a day off.

"What kind of food would you like for your winter picnic?" he queried. Eva smiled.

"Champagne, caviar, you know the posh stuff."

"What about a hot dog?" Henrik laughed as he picked Alfie up for a cuddle. "Do you want to come with us, little man?"

"Where are you going?" John asked as he entered the kitchen.

"Hi John, we are off to Monte Faito for a snowball fight. Do you want to come?"

"Sounds like fun, but I'll leave it to you, young people. I've got plans for the vineyard today."

"Do you mind if we take Alfie? I think he wants to come with us." Henrik said as he watched the little dog heading straight for the back of the van.

"I'm sure he will love that. Hold on, I'll get his winter coat Martha brought him for Christmas. He'll need it up there."

A short while later, they were heading up the winding road to Monte Faito starting from Castellammare.

"I was reading about Monte Faito," Henrik said. "It's quite an interesting place. Not only can you see the Bay of Naples, Ischia, Procida, and Capri. Apparently, there is a 10th-century temple on the summit, the Sanctuary of San Michele. The birch trees grown here have always been used for boat building, but what is fascinating is the ice traders used to transport the snow down to the Neapolitan nobles to keep their wine cooled."

"Wow! This whole area is amazing. Don't you think? There is so much to discover. I'm so glad we live here, and as soon as we can, we must visit Pompeii and Herculaneum. Last year, we didn't have a moment, did we?"

"We should take time to discover more about the area especially the history. It could encourage people to come and visit. Look, I think we are here. I'll park in the car park, and then we can take our picnic with us into the woods. What do you think?"

Eva glanced around. The trees were dripping with soft snow, enticing visitors to venture into the woods to enjoy the enchanting wonderland that snow always conjures up.

"Yes, that sounds really magical. Come on,

Alfie, food time."

Alfie was bursting with energy and excitement as they let him out of the back of the van. He was off in an instant, discovering the joy of ice-cold snow. Henrik and Eva tried in vain to grab him to put his waterproof coat on. They quickly put their boots on and rushed off to rein him in. It wasn't long before they were also rolling around in the snow. The snowball fight that Henrik had initiated had developed into a power game. Eva, in defeat, lay on the floor doing 'snow angels' while Alfie jumped on her.

After a while, they calmed down and took in their surroundings. The views were amazing.

"Honestly, you wouldn't believe we are in Italy. It's more like Canada or North America." Eva said as she took photographs of the tall trees draped in cobwebs of ice and snow. "You know, Henrik, this place needs a wood cabin in the middle of the trees with a big log fire and someone making hot apple and cinnamon pie, and ice cream. Wouldn't that be great?"

"Eva, you are always thinking about food. Mind

you, it's a brilliant idea. We'll have to look into it. We could get someone to run it for us in the winter, and in the summer, we could turn it into an iced pudding cafe. We could be the first to introduce English and Danish sweet recipes, like frozen snowball pudding!"

Eva laughed. "I don't know who has the biggest imagination, you or me. We'll check it out. Are you hungry? Shall we have our picnic on the bench over there? "

A loud bark of agreement from Alfie made them laugh.

"I'm really enjoying today, Henrik. It's been so special, and I will always remember this moment." Eva said as she poured two small glasses of Prosecco. "Let's toast happiness and good health for everyone this year."

Henrik looked at the sky. He smiled as tiny snowflakes began to drift down from the clouds to add to this perfect moment. He moved towards her as he took the glasses from her hand and placed them on the bench, quickly sweeping her into his arms. A long lingering kiss was their toast to the New Year.

"Eva," he said as he knelt in the snow and revealed a tiny box he held in his hand. "Eva, I love you and want to spend the rest of my life with you. Gift dig med mig? (marry me?)"

"What," Eva said. "I don't understand?"

"We should get married. Please say yes and be my wife?"

Her initial reaction was of total surprise and then delight spread over her face.

"Yes... I mean Ja." She melted into his open arms, and they held each other for a long time.

"Oh, Henrik, this ring is beautiful." She looked at the small diamond solitaire. "It looks like a piece of ice. I love you so much." The emotion of this magical moment started to well up in her heart.

"I bought it at Christmas. I was going to propose then, but we didn't get much time to ourselves with my family, so I've been carrying it with me, waiting for the right moment." He looked around him. "And this is it!"

"A snow ring." Eva laughed.

Henrik picked Alfie up, who was looking at both of them and wondering why they didn't want to play anymore. "We are getting married, Alfie. She loves me. She loves me! He kissed the small dog on his nose, and they started running around in the snow! Eva joined him, holding the two glasses.

"A new toast ... to love." She said as she passed him a glass. "This is the most wonderful day of my life."

"Me too," Henrik replied as he drank his wine. "Shall we fill this champagne glass with snow as a present for Martha?"

"What a great idea, she will love it. We can keep it in the freezer box. I can't wait to see her face when we tell her we are getting married, and there will be another wedding to plan!"

A couple of hours later, the young couple, immersed in their happiness bubble, arrived at The Villa eager to share their news.

"Look, that's Dr. Rossi's car. I wonder what he is doing here?" Eva said as Henrik parked the van and opened the door to allow Alfie to jump out and head straight for the kitchen, his tail wagging madly.

"Alfie. Vieni qui," (come here). Martha shouted. "Look at him; he's so wet! Come, darling, get close to the fire." Alfie didn't need any telling. Already, he was making himself comfortable in his bed by the flickering flames. He was totally exhausted.

"Hi, what's going on? Has something happened?"

"Oh Eva, Henrik, come in. Samantha has some news, and I'm afraid it's not very good."

"I've just been telling everyone that Lorenzo and I are heading up to the hospital in Bergamo in Lombardy. They are overwhelmed with cases of this new virus and are appealing for medics. We've been asked if we could go and help. So I've just returned to pack a bag, and we are driving up tonight."

"Oh no, that sounds serious," Eva said.

"We don't know yet. There is little information about the virus except it is a respiratory illness. The word is that it is very contagious and has no cure, so the experts are worried it might become a pandemic, although it's early days."

Samantha's words suddenly penetrated Eva's thoughts.

"You mean it could affect tourism and our business?"

Samantha moved to hug Eva.

"We don't know yet. It's all new, but the sooner we act, the sooner we can prevent it from getting out of hand. I'm sorry we must go. I'm so glad I saw you before we went. It may be some time before we can come back."

"Samantha, my darling, please take care of yourself and Lorenzo." Martha, her voice showing concern, went to give her a hug. "It sounds quite dangerous, and please let us know what is happening."

"Don't worry, we will try to avoid large crowds. I don't want any of you to get ill. So, keep listening to the news broadcasts. Oh, and say goodbye to Mary and Franco for us. Sorry, we missed them."

"We will. Now you get off and drive carefully." John picked up her bags and carried them to the car.

"Well, that's bad news," John said when he returned to the kitchen. "It could be devastating for the tourist industry and the restaurant."

"We mustn't panic. It is early days." Martha said. "Although I do hope Samantha and Lorenzo will be safe. I've lived through war and various disease outbreaks, but a pandemic means worldwide. It sounds frightening. Anyway, I suggest we carry on and make contingency plans as we understand more."

She turned to Eva and Henrik and changing the subject she asked.

"How was Monte Faito, darling? Did you have fun? I can see that Alfie has."

"It was amazing, wasn't it, Henrik? And we've brought you a little present back."

Henrik opened the freezer bag and was pleased to see the snow hadn't melted in the glass.

Martha laughed. "This is the most thoughtful present I've ever had. Snow from the top of Monte Faito. Thank you so much."

Alfie suddenly woke up, and Martha rubbed snow on his nose.

"It was amazing, Martha. The views are incredible, and it was so quiet and romantic up there."

"Of course, it is the perfect combination for magic to happen." Martha said.

At this point, Eva thought it might be the best moment to announce their engagement. She was hoping to tell her father first. Still, Henrik had said to her that Franco knew. He had happily agreed they should marry on one condition: that Henrik didn't take his daughter away.

With a moment of shyness, Eva quietly said, "Martha, John, we have some news for you." And she slowly held out her left hand so they could see her engagement ring.

A squeal of delight from Martha and 'congratulations' from John followed by the sound of the champagne cork as it pinged around the kitchen. All thoughts of a pandemic quickly disappeared from their mind.

Coronavirus
(Il Coronavirus)

The traffic heading north on the autostrada to Rome was extremely busy. Samantha rested her head on the luxurious leather headrest of Lorenzo's Maserati car and sighed deeply.

"Stai bene, Sam?" (Are you OK?) He asked. "You are not having second thoughts, are you?"

"No, not at all. It is the right thing to do, but I am worried I don't have enough experience to help. It's all so unknown."

"It is for all of us. Unfortunately, we can only go with the information we have. But we must protect ourselves. That is our first priority. I would never forgive myself if anything happened to you."

"I feel the same for you," she said as she glanced at him. His handsome features now visibly displaying signs of worry. "We just have to be sensible and not take risks. In fact, I'll make a list of things we might need." She reached into her handbag for a notebook and pen and noticed she had a message coming through on her phone

"Lorenzo, you'll never guess what's happened. When they went to Monte Faito this morning, Henrik proposed to Eva, and she said yes. Oh, I'm so pleased."

"Quanto brillante - (how brilliant) they are perfect for each other. It is wonderful when two people fall in love, and they only have eyes for each other."

Sam glanced at Lorenzo; she was puzzled by his tone of voice. There was a hint of sadness in him.

"They are the perfect couple, young with their whole lives ahead of them, and it helps to have the same interests, don't you agree? Many people think they are in love but have very little in common with each other, and then things fall apart." He said.

"Or things happen in life, and it changes everything. I suppose we are about to experience how resilient we are as humans." Samantha replied.

"And how caring. In times of difficulty, people find how deep their emotions go. Suddenly, what we thought was important isn't anymore." Lorenzo moved to the fast lane, and Samantha viewed the changing scenery.

"I do wonder what is in store for us all. An unknown virus sounds quite frightening. It could be devastating for the world. How has it happened? Do you think nature is trying to balance us out, or is it something more sinister?'

"I don't know, Sam. I hope it is not intentional. We certainly don't need more aggression. There is so much poverty and fighting in the world. If you add an unknown virus to the mix, it will be hard to control. To be honest, it is the last thing the world needs."

"It's funny, but I'm looking at the most stunning scenery in a beautiful country full of culture and colour. Here, we are talking almost as if the world is under threat. It's hard to believe. You know last year was very difficult for me. When Robbie died, I thought I would never recover. I wanted to die too, but I couldn't hurt my family, so I ended up here in this most wonderful country, looking for a place I knew my husband loved to lay him to rest.

And also to find some peace for myself."

"And you did. Your life has changed. It's moved on, hasn't it?"

"It certainly changed. Meeting Martha and having this amazing opportunity to be part of something special has helped enormously. Deep down, I have accepted Robbie's death. Although I still don't understand why he, of all people, should become ill. He was so fit and young."

"There is no logic or reason to it. I've seen so many times when life has been suddenly taken away. We have to prepare ourselves for some heartache. It may be an unknown journey ahead of us, Sam."

"I know, and don't worry about me. I will do my best, and I can cope. I couldn't rest knowing I hadn't even tried."

Lorenzo turned off the autostrada. "Let's stop for some food and a break. We have at least another four hours of driving ahead of us."

She smiled. "That sounds like a great idea."

Samantha looked around the café. It was full of people, and she wondered where everyone was going. Looking at their faces, she could see them living their day-to-day life, unaware of the dangers ahead.

Lorenzo placed a tray of sandwiches and coffee on the table. They silently sipped their drinks. Both seemed unable to eat very much and just picked at their food.

"This is all happening so quickly," Sam said. "It was only a few weeks ago we were celebrating Mary and Franco's wedding, and now look at us. Those people over there are having a good time yet don't know what is ahead."

"It is strange, Sam. I am trying to understand how it has happened so quickly."

Lorenzo looked at the young woman. His heart felt a sudden surge of love. So strong were his feelings for her. He admired her strength of character, especially overcoming the death of her husband at such a young age. His dream would be to eventually come together to get to know each other more. Still, this situation was certainly different from what he had in mind. In fact, he had planned a special Valentine's surprise for her, but now that was cancelled, and it didn't seem appropriate to mention it.

"I think I've had enough to eat, Lorenzo. Shall we get going?"

"Si, the sooner we are there, the better."

They headed for the car and the onward journey north. They may have considered turning around and heading south if they had a tiny glimpse of what was in store.

***

As soon as Samantha and Lorenzo arrived in Bergamo, they immediately started work. The hospital, although appearing to be in chaos, was managing to cope, but only just. They were both horrified to be told that the medical staff were dealing with over 800 confirmed cases of COVID-19.

Lorenzo turned to Samantha.

"I've been asked to help in the emergency department. Do you think you will be OK, Sam? I understand if you want to change your mind."

"I'm not even considering that. There is work to be done, and if I can help, I will do my best. Just make sure that you look after yourself. Don't be a hero."

She watched him walk down the corridor towards the quarantine wards. The realisation of this situation was suddenly becoming a reality. They were both potentially in danger, but then, looking around at the desperate state of the staff, some crying, others so worn out that they had fallen asleep where they had rested for a moment, she knew that she had no choice.

Sam was welcomed by a senior nurse and was quickly introduced to the staff. They asked if she could help with any translation problems, and they directed her to a ward that was being prepared to be a makeshift care unit. With a quick glance out of the window, Sam could see the erection of temporary emergency tents for new patients to be assessed before being moved to the wards. The situation she now found herself in felt like a war zone. But there was no time to be frightened. Just like everyone else, she would be learning as she went along.

They were both thrown in at the deep end and before they realised what was happening, each day began to merge into the next. Sleep was a necessity but was taken as and when time allowed. They settled into a routine and rarely saw each other except in the restroom or canteen.

"How is it going, Sam?" Lorenzo asked her when they bumped into each other at the end of a very stressful night.

"I have never seen anything like this before," Sam said. "It's so frustrating. All these people are very poorly, and we can only do so much to help them."

"I know. I lost three patients in the night, and I just feel with better knowledge of the virus, I could have done more to save them. Have you heard the rumour that there may be a vaccine in a few months?"

"Really! That will be amazing, but surely it is too soon?"

"I don't know, but we must keep hoping. I'm so

glad you are OK. I've missed you and feel guilty for dragging you up here."

"Lorenzo, you couldn't have stopped me. I'm fine. The only problem I have is with these horrible masks. They are really tight around my head."

"I agree. They are unbearable." He looked at Samantha. "When this is over, I will take you somewhere beautiful to compensate for it."

She laughed. "I will hold you to that."

"I'll see you back at the apartment soon. Take care, Sam. I must go, but make sure you get some sleep. You look tired."

"So do you. Bye, Lorenzo. Keep safe."

They parted company, but both felt an overwhelming concern for each other. Lorenzo wanted to rush and grab hold of Samantha and take her away from this nightmare. Somewhere safe and beautiful where, he would make passionate love to her, and she would respond without any feeling of guilt or regret. As for Sam, her emotions were so intense she couldn't make sense of them. She needed time, and that was something neither of them had. She turned briefly to watch him walk down the corridor, and at that moment, he, too, turned. They waved silently, a simple gesture that held a lot of meaning, much like a hug or caress, and even more poignant as this was denied to everybody.

The temporary accommodation they had been given was in an apartment block near the hospital. A small two-bed flat had been put at their disposal. So far, Samantha had only spent a few nights there. She had bought some food so Lorenzo could eat if he needed to. But she didn't think he had left the hospital during the weeks they had been there.

***

A month after their arrival, Samantha had been working very long hours. She was due eight hours off but continued until the ward sister insisted she go home to rest.

"Samantha, you are no good to us if you don't

get some sleep. Andare a casa (go home)"

It was with a heavy heart she headed back to their flat. Standing under the hot shower, she allowed the water to flow over her to ease the pain in her head. It felt wonderful, like a tropical waterfall in some far-off land. The physical pain she could cope with, but the visual images of people struggling to breathe were hard to erase from her mind. One after another, newly diagnosed patients came through the hospital. A few were helped with breathing, but many were taken to intensive care, where Lorenzo worked.

Samantha's job was to look after the less infected. Even so, it was a struggle to help people relax to enable them to breathe more easily. Panic became their first reaction, but Samantha had a calming effect. Her voice became almost hypnotic as she quickly learnt that language was not a barrier, but kindness and caring were equally effective in instilling confidence in her patients. In particular, she was drawn to the very elderly and young adults who needed family support but could not have it. She sat for long periods comforting frightened elderly people. It was heartbreaking to see them suffer and yet offer very little in the way of hope.

As a professional nurse, she had experience of keeping her own feelings under control, but she soon realised that fear of the disease was beginning to affect her. After seeing the suffering it was causing, she was extra cautious about her safety. Twice this week, she had been physically sick. She had to force herself to eat, as food was the last thing on her mind. It would be so easy to hug a patient who desperately needed contact, but she knew that wasn't advised. Still, she was unsure of the safety equipment, which didn't seem adequate. She was a nurse, and it was all in the hands of fate whether she would succumb to this illness. She headed to her bedroom, and for once, she relaxed and gave in to the overwhelming feeling of exhaustion.

After a deep sleep, Samantha woke to a darkened room. At first, she didn't know if it was night or day. The air in the flat was stifling. Stepping out onto the tiny balcony to breathe in the freshness of the night, she realised that life was all about breathing. From the moment you took your first breath as you came into the world until you departed with a faint gasping last breath, desperate to cling on to life and then nothing.

The church bell chimed at 2 a.m. The streets were lifeless, devoid of humans, except for a lonely cat wandering the road, searching for food and contact with somebody ... anybody.

Never in her life had she experienced such loneliness. The tears began to fall silently down her face. She cried out for Lorenzo, but her heart was aching for Robbie. If only he was here. She needed him now more than at any time in their relationship.

Slowly, in the distance, she could hear the heartbreaking sounds of a lone singer. His voice began softly, filling the night air with beauty and hope.

'It's a sign,' she whispered to herself. She recognised the aria. It was one of Robbie's favourite pieces *'Your tiny hand is frozen*." He used to say, *'Listen to this, Sam, it is from*

Puccini's finest opera, La Boheme.' Tonight, it seemed so poignant. Suddenly, she didn't feel so alone.

People opened their shutters and came out onto their balconies to listen. Italy, the country of passion, love, and music, had been starved of this happiness, and yet it took a lone singer to open his heart to the world to express his sorrow. When he had finished, loud applause rang out down the cobbled streets like music caressing the ancient buildings and filling the town with love.

A noise distracted her. It came from the kitchen, and upon opening the door, she found Lorenzo, his body slumped over the table with his head in his hands.

"Lorenzo, stai bene? (are you OK?") she asked gently.

He lifted his head, "Ciao, Sam, Si sto bene, (yes I'm fine.) Just tired. They sent me home to sleep."

"You look worn out. Go to bed. I'll bring you a hot drink and some food."

"Yes, I will, just for a little while."

It wasn't long before Lorenzo was deeply asleep. Samantha checked on him before going back to the hospital. His food lay uneaten on the bedside table.

Covid Lockdown
(Confinamento per il Covid)

John had spent the morning pruning shoots on the vines in preparation for the growing season. He was pleasantly tired. It was backbreaking but necessary to achieve his dream of producing a decent wine.

When he entered the sitting room he was surprised to see everyone gathered round the television.

"You are just in time," Mary said. "There is a special announcement from the Government about the crisis."

"That doesn't sound good," John said as he sat on the arm of the sofa.

They listened silently as they were informed that Coronavirus was spreading rapidly throughout the country, and every area had reported new cases. The only option left to the Government was to lock the country down immediately to keep everyone safe. Residents were told to stay home except for essential work and medical reasons and not to mix with people. Hygiene was a top priority, and hand sanitizers and facemasks would soon be available. Airports would be closed in 48 hours until further notice.

Henrik looked across to see Eva's reaction. She was visibly shaken and trying to take in this information and the effect it would have on them.

"This changes everything," she cried. "All our hard work last year and our plans for the future have gone."

Henrik went to console her.

"We don't know what the future holds." He whispered in her ear. "But we have to be practical and positive."

"But we will have to close the restaurant for the foreseeable future." Her voice raised in fear.

"Hold on," John said. Eva, you are overreacting. This is all new to us, but scientists will look at the situation and come up with a solution. It won't be the first time the world has encountered an unknown virus. Look at the plague or the flu pandemic. We understand a lot more about these kinds of diseases. I'm sure it won't be long before they come up with an answer."

Eva suddenly started to cry. Henrik was alarmed. She was always so positive and optimistic.

"Don't be afraid, Eva. We will get through this, I promise."

"But where has it come from? Are we all going to die?"

The room became silent; everyone was wondering precisely the same thing.

"This is the only thing the government can do," Mary said. I know it stops our reopening, but this virus is a killer, and our first priority is keeping everyone safe. So we must adhere to the advice and stay home away from people. We must also remain positive. It is early days."

Martha spoke quietly. "I do hope Samantha is safe. I'm beginning to worry we haven't heard from her."

"I thought the same. I messaged Sam earlier to ask her to put our minds at rest," Eva said.

"They did show the hospital in Bergamo on the television. It's like a war zone, with people lying in the corridors, unable to breathe. So, I'm not surprised she hasn't had a moment to respond to us. She must be worn out." John said.

Eva's phone pinged.

"She must have heard me! It's Sam. Apparently, the situation is serious, but do not worry about her. They have been told about the lockdown and said we must all stay safe. Her job is to care for the not-so-urgent cases, and Lorenzo is on the front line in the emergency units. She is worried about Lorenzo. He's been working hard and refuses to take proper rest."

"Ask her to keep us updated and let her know we are sending lots of love to both of them," Mary said. "Oh, and tell her we are looking after each other because I know she will worry."

"Will do,"

"And Eva, tell her we miss her and to keep safe."

Eva relayed the message. A few minutes later,

they were in the kitchen making a list of what they needed to do.

"First of all." John said. "We must cancel our wedding bookings, although everywhere is experiencing the same problems as Italy. It is a matter of taking each day as it comes. Then, all the other events we had planned will go on hold. There isn't a lot we can do until we know how long the lockdown will go on. What are the accounts looking like, Mary? How long can we go without any income coming in?"

"As you all know, last year we had an amazing year. But the profits have gone back into The Villa on the vineyard, gardens, equipment, etc. That said Martha has paid for all the renovation work on the bedrooms. We are in profit and probably OK for two or three months."

Martha joined in the conversation.

"We could provide a service for the town. People need to eat, and we will have grown a lot of vegetables from the gardens that will go to waste unless we use them."

"Oh, I know what we can do," Eva said, "Henrik and I can bake bread and maybe have a stall in Piazza Tasso if we can get permission. We could have an honesty box and charge a small fee to cover costs."

"What about a takeaway service? We could order some packaging and do pizzas or even meals?" Henrik suggested.

"It's a good idea." Mary interrupted. "I'll see what Franco is doing regarding his fishermen. I suppose that comes under essential work."

"You know, years ago, the fishermen used to go from one apartment building to another, selling their catch of the day. Women used to lower baskets on a rope with money, and the fishermen would put the wrapped up fish in the basket, and then it was hoisted up. We could do the same to get vegetables and food to the people stuck in their homes. That way, we wouldn't be putting people at risk with physical contact. What do you all think?"

'Well, I, for one, think it is a great idea, Martha." John said. We can be really inventive and use our time and energy to help. Besides, if we have masks and don't go near people, we should be OK."

"I agree, John," Martha replied as she headed for the door. "I'm just going to telephone the monastery to inform them about the lockdown. They probably haven't heard the news. I'll make sure they have enough food. Perhaps, John, we could leave some fresh bread outside their door each day? They have a minimal diet, mainly the vegetables they grow, but I'm sure they would appreciate some fresh bread."

"It's a good idea, Martha. It will make us all feel better if we have something positive to do. Otherwise, we will get depressed and worry about the situation." Mary said. Her mind was buzzing with practical ideas. She loved a challenge, although maybe a dangerous virus wasn't what she had in mind.

Martha turned to John. "Another thing I must do today is to arrange a meeting with the management of my hotel to inform the staff that we have to close immediately. I wonder if you would come with me, John?"

"Of course I will. There is so much to think about. It's good the Government will cover their earnings while they are off work."

"Yes, we'll see how that goes. I can afford to top their wages up a bit. My staff have been loyal and worked for my family for many years. In fact, I will ask Signor Miccio to come and stay with us. He has no family and has only lived in rooms in the hotel. I don't like the idea of him being alone at a time like this."

"He will jump at the chance, Martha. He is going to be so disappointed the hotel is closing. He won't know what to do with himself."

"Good. I'm feeling much better now I have a plan. He can have one of the new bedrooms."

"It will be great having him around," Eva said. "He's been an inspiration to Henrik and me in the kitchen. I often think if I had a granddad, I would like him to have been Signor Miccio."

"I wonder if he knows anything about growing grapes?" John asked,

"I think he knows a good vintage when he drinks it," Martha laughed.

Lockdown Anxiety

(Ansia da Blocco)

Coronavirus has affected everyone in different ways. Samantha and Lorenzo, being medically trained, had, without hesitation, felt they had a duty to help sick people. Of course, they were concerned for their safety, but no one could have persuaded either to stay home.

Francesco and Mary were catapulted out of their 'honeymoon' bubble. Franco was apprehensive about how he could continue to pay his fishermen. The hotels were facing closure, so there would be little demand for the high volume of fish his men caught. It was a huge relief to him when the Government announced measures to provide monetary funding to supplement workers' incomes.

Franco decided he would take the fishing boat out at night and sell the catch to the residents in Sorrento. He was kept busy with his scaled-down business.

Meanwhile, Eva reacted badly to the closure of the restaurant. Her reaction surprised Henrik, but he soon understood how important the last year had been to her. And they spent a long time discussing Eva's childhood compared to his own.

"When this is all over, I think we should take a trip to see my folks in Copenhagen," Henrik said as they tried adjusting to the lockdown and what it had meant to them.

"But what if it doesn't end, Henrik? Our lives have changed in an instant. I don't understand how you can be so calm about it. We could all die!"

"Eva, what is wrong with you? It's not like you to be so negative."

"I'm scared." She said and suddenly burst into tears again.

"Oh, Eva, come here." He gave her a big hug. "I know it's scary; it is for all of us, but we have to accept it and try and work out how best we can get through. Life will be back to normal one day soon. Trust me."

"But you can't promise that. Look, I'm not a child. I'm so afraid that you, Martha, or any of us will get ill. Everything we worked hard for last year has stopped overnight. You've just asked me to marry you. One minute, my life felt perfect. I'd found my father, and I had fallen in love with you, and the next minute it's all gone!"

Henrik looked at her. He could see her fear. Her normally happy face and soft brown eyes that expressed all her feelings suddenly looked drained, like someone had switched a light off. How can he help her with this? He desperately wanted to marry her right now. What had attracted her to him from the very beginning was her positive attitude to life. Finding out her mother had deceived her and then being left alone in the world at 17, just when life should be fun and exciting. She had turned to her inner self and strength and gone to Italy to make a new life. She was strong, didn't need anybody, and would survive whatever happened. But suddenly, she showed her vulnerability, and he wasn't sure what to do.

"Eva, listen to me. Look at all you have gone through in the last few years. This virus is just another hurdle for you to jump over. We live in a modern world, where medical research and technology will be on to this immediately. We aren't living in medieval times. It may seem like a plague, but we will soon have a vaccine. Everything is going to be all right."

"Yes, of course, you are right. I'm just being silly. I'll pull myself together. I don't want to let you down."

"You are not letting me down. Please don't think that. We are in this together. We just need to calm down and get practical, as always. So when you are ready, we'll make a list. I like lists. It gives me order, things to tick off, and a plan."

She laughed, "I like lists too." She kissed him. "Come on, let's go outside while we can and go down to the cove. We can look at Mount Vesuvius and reminisce about our picnic on Monte Faito and your lovely proposal."

"Sounds like a good idea. We can discuss our wedding too. There is much to look forward to and make arrangements. Our website needs updating. We are responsible to our followers to be positive and spread hope so they may come and visit us soon."

"Come on then, I'll put my boots on. Some fresh air will be good. Thanks, Henrik. I feel much better."

***

John is also struggling with his thoughts. He is standing on the terrace overlooking the Bay of Naples. Mount Vesuvius, the iconic volcano, is staring back at him. A thin white cloud hovers over the snow-capped crater, giving the illusion that the mighty beast is still alive and kicking and churning smoke.

'Not your time, is it, old man?' John says to the mountain. *'I know you are pretending to be dead to put us at ease, but we know what you are up to. Inside that fat belly of yours, you are creating fire and purgatory. You are building up for another onslaught of despair and disaster.'* John gives a

loud, sardonic laugh. A thought occurs to him that humanity is being tested. What would be a worse way to die? Being smothered by molten ash and fire and turned to stone like the poor souls in Pompeii? Or dying slowly, unable to expel air, as the body drowns internally from an unknown virus that is threatening to destroy the world?

A vision appears in his mind. Another way to leave this life would be as a result of war. His face becomes contorted with anger. He remembers his army life, the enemy's eyes as they came face to face, and the look of horror as he pulled the trigger and they fell to their death. And then he remembers Giovanni, the young man who had killed himself so violently by jumping off the cliff in front of him. *'No, I can't think about that now. I just can't.'* He turns back to the mighty volcano.

'Enjoy your power over this beautiful place. I have no doubt your day will come, and you will erupt again with ash and fire and destroy all our hopes and dreams just like this virus is trying to do.'

He walks away, his PTSD affecting him badly today. His body is aching with bitterness and hate. He looks down at Alfie, who is staring up at him with such love in his eyes that John immediately hugs him and allows the soothing presence of his little dog to work its magic and calm him down.

Grand Hotel Italia

(Grand Hotel Italia)

The Grand Hotel Italia had been the pride and joy of Martha's family. They owned an old building in Sorrento, and in the mid-fifties, her parents decided to borrow money and renovate it, offering accommodation for wealthy visitors who were beginning to travel again in search of beautiful scenery. The area was slowly recovering from the devastation of the war, and in later years, after the death of her parents, her twin brothers, Paulo and John Franco, had run the hotel together. Sadly, they had both passed away within a few months of each other, leaving Martha alone to inherit the hotel.

John drove to the side entrance and parked in Martha's private parking lot. He helped her out.

'Do you want me to wait for you?" he asked.

"No, John, come in with me. I need your moral support. This is a situation I haven't come across before, and I'm not looking forward to it."

They entered the large reception area, and the

manager, Tonino Conti greeted them with outstretched arms.

"Signora, Benvenuta (welcome). It is always a pleasure to see you, but sadly, I know why you are here today."

"It is indeed difficult times, Tonino. As you are expecting, the hotel will not be opening for the summer season. The virus is spreading rapidly throughout Europe, and air travel is cancelled. We can only assume things will get worse before they get better. I understand the Government will pay basic wages for the staff. I want you to impress upon them that I value their service and their jobs will be safe. I will look into topping up their wages. I don't want anyone to worry. We will have to monitor carefully throughout this year to see whether it is feasible to reopen the hotel when lockdown is lifted. If the tourists cannot fly, it will be necessary to keep the hotel closed. Anyway, we shall have to assess the situation as it happens."

Tonino nodded.

"Do you require a skeleton staff to look after

the property?"

"Yes, we could ask for volunteers. Shall I leave that for you to organise?

"Yes, of course. I know one or two members of staff who will be willing to do that."

"Grazie. Now, I would like a word with Signor Miccio. Could you kindly get him for me?"

"Si, of course. Please, Signora, take a seat in the lounge. Can I get you a drink? Perhaps some coffee?"

"No, thank you, Tonino. I don't want to hold you up. I'm sure you have a lot to organise."

Signor Conti hurried away, leaving Martha to rest momentarily in the beautifully decorated lounge. The hotel was something she was very proud of. It held many memories for her, especially as, in the early days, this was where she first met George and where their love had blossomed.

A tear formed in her eye and she swallowed quickly to physically draw on her inner strength. Grief was always with her, but she was learning to accept it and to control her emotions. It helped to believe George was by her side, silently guiding her until they would be together again.

Meanwhile, John was wandering around the hotel. He vividly remembered his stay here only last year when his life was on the brink of disaster. He was almost bankrupt, and his future looked grim. How the world had changed. He sighed. *'It's ironic,"* he thought *'just when everything looked so rosy, this had to happen.'* All he wanted to do was work hard, nurture and love the vineyard, and produce something creative again with his hands. He still enjoyed making his range of leather goods for the local boutiques, which always pleased him, but the vineyard was a new venture and exciting. He saw Martha beckoning him, and he quickly joined her.

Signor Miccio was also rushing to meet his employer in the sitting room.

"Bouongiorno Signor. I wanted a word with you about the pandemic."

"Bouongiorno Signora, it is a pleasure to see you."

"As you may have realised we cannot open the

hotel this season, and I am a little concerned for your welfare. Would you like to come and stay at The Villa? We have a nice room you could have and, as we will all be in lockdown, we can ensure we are looking after each other. How would you like that?"

Signor Miccio grasped at his heart. He was so overwhelmed by his employer's generosity and kindness. He was momentarily lost for words.

Martha could tell by his emotional reaction he was touched. To cover up his embarrassment, she quickly suggested they could take him back now if he wanted to pack a suitcase. He promptly agreed and rushed off, saying he would be very quick.

John smiled at Martha.

"You are a very kind woman. I think you have made his day."

"It's nothing, John. I cannot bear to think of him alone in this hotel. He needs people around him. And this situation must be frightening for someone who has no relatives. I am delighted he will join us, and everyone will make a big fuss of him."

"They will indeed. You know, Martha, you have this hotel just right. The colour scheme is soft but relaxing, and the entrance to the hotel with the long marble tunnel is simply stunning. It must have cost a fortune to build."

It did, John, but the original entrance was on a busy street and didn't enhance the hotel. Now, with the long tunnel and the fun of getting the golf buggy to take you up the main entrance, it's pretty thrilling. Well worth the money. And it is something no other hotel in Sorrento has."

"I like how you have built the gardens into the cliff face. The lovely statues and lemon trees are just stunning. It reminds me of an oil painting. It is such a shame everything is closing down. I can't imagine somewhere as vibrant as Sorrento to be suddenly empty of people. I understand how Signor Micchio feels."

"Ah, here he comes. Could you help him with his luggage? He doesn't seem to have very much."

"Of course I will. Yes, let's all go home. Have

you finished with your business?"

"Yes, John. The management will close the hotel and keep a staff member checking the rooms daily. I'm feeling quite sad about it all. I am so glad my father isn't here to see what is happening.

"Don't worry, Martha. I'm sure it is temporary. The important thing is that we keep well so we can reopen and welcome the world back here when the time is right. It will happen."

"Thank you, John. I know you are right."

***

Signor Miccio was welcomed into The Villa with so much enthusiasm he almost cried. Eva insisted he sat in the kitchen as she prepared some food for him. John took his bags to one of the newly decorated rooms.

"Signor Miccio, I am so happy you are staying with us. I hope you will teach me some of the tricks of running a successful restaurant." Eva smiled as she placed a plate of Frutti di Mare (seafood pasta) before him.

"Signorina, how did you know this is my favourite dish?"

"I didn't, but I'm glad you like it."

Henrik stepped forward, holding a bottle of white wine.

"Vino, Signor?" he asked as he smiled broadly.

"Grazie, A perfect compliment to such delicious food."

Henrik sat next to him. "I wonder if you would be happy to be part of our podcast on social media. Eva and I have a website dedicated to the restaurant, but it would be wonderful if you would let us interview you as a successful restaurateur and tell us about your amazing experiences."

"I have little knowledge of technical things, but I would be more than happy to pass on my experiences of which I have many."

"Brilliant, Signor. We will guide you; you don't have to worry about anything. Just be aware that you may become quite famous online, especially if you allow us to film you singing. You are a brilliant personality and will be a real asset to promoting The Villa and the hotel when everything returns to normal."

"Indeed. I am grateful for anything I can do to add to this amazing place. As you know, it has been a pleasure to come here and be part of everything."

Eva interrupted. "And now you are living here. It is going to be such fun."

Wine Cellar

(Cantina)

"Follow me, John," Martha said as she led him down the path to the wine cellar. Nature had created an archway of tangled ivy, making the area dark but strangely beautiful, as though time had stood still until this moment.

"This needs a good sort out," John said as he pulled away at the overgrowth to allow Martha to reach the oak door.

"It's years since I have been down here. I have no idea what we will find. My father and George spent many hours in here distilling wine," she laughed, "or rather drinking it."

Eventually, the door gave way with some heavy shoving from John. It creaked open, and Martha reached inside for the light switch.

"My goodness, I didn't think this would still work," she said as the flickering lights revealed a large stone room.

"This is stunning, Martha," John's eyes took in the creamy soft colour of the stonework and the magnificent vaulted ceiling.

They couldn't resist touching the old wine bottles as they walked around. The dust settled on their hands like tiny particles of time.

"We can do a lot with this room. Turning it into a cheese and wine-tasting experience is a great idea. We could have a music evening with a guitar player. It could be quite popular. I suggest filling the room with candles and soft lighting and inviting Signor Miccio to belt out a few songs."

"He would love that, John. It would make an excellent venue for a musical evening. Martha picked up a dusty bottle of red wine from the wooden rack. She glanced at the label.

"Oh, I remember this. My father drew the design. Look, John, it was the first vintage that he produced. My goodness, this takes me back. He was so proud of it."

"What a find. There are lots more over here."

John moved across the dusty wooden floor. A ray of sunlight streamed through a broken skylight directly onto the corner of the room. Something had caught his eye. A reflection bouncing off a broken cabinet revealed what looked like a door.

"What's this, Martha? It looks like there is another room."

"It leads down some stairs to my father's office. Here, let me help you move this cabinet."

"No, don't worry. I can move it later. It's very dusty in here. I'll get some cleaning things and give it a good sweep out. It is fascinating, though. Just think what an addition it will be to The Villa. It would be amazing, and even more so, if we could produce a new wine. I can't wait for that to happen. We'll certainly have a big party."

"Oh, John, what a moment that will be our own vintage. I can't wait to taste it."

"Well, that's settled then. I'll get it cleared out. The floorboards are in good condition. It needs a few nails here and there, and the stonework could do with de-cobwebbing; although I like it, it adds to the character. I'll make a start this afternoon."

***

After lunch, John returned to the wine cellar keen to start work, although the room seemed reasonably clean and tidy, bearing in mind its years of neglect. It was only a short time before he had worked his way around to the old wooden cabinet. He pushed it to one side to reveal a padlocked door. The wooden panels were worn, and the lock came away quickly. He opened the door, which revealed stone steps leading to a dark and dismal room. John fumbled for a light switch. 'Wow,' he said. 'It's like going back in time.' He looked around. A large desk stood in the centre of the room. On the dusty leather top stood an old lamp.

Sitting at the desk, John opened the drawers and pulled out a leather-bound book. Flipping through the pages, he could see recordings of volume and sales for each variety of wine the vineyard had produced over decades until the death of Signor Russo, Martha's father. It was challenging to read as the paper had become pale and illegible with age. John smiled as he saw the red rim mark of a wine glass on a number of the pages. Obviously, there had been a few glasses of wine drunk during the recordings of the grape harvest. He could almost sense the family's excitement when they had a successful year. This is what he wanted to feel more than anything. The thrill of growing and lovingly caring for his grapes until the time to pick and bottle his own vintage, pour a glass, inhale the bouquet, and put it to his lips must be the most fantastic feeling. Finding this wine cellar made him even more determined to follow his dream and one day be sitting at this desk and recording his first successful vintage in this magnificent ledger.

The sound of Alfie barking brought John back to reality.

"What's up," John shouted as he headed over to see what his little dog was doing.

Alfie looked up an expression on his face of being caught doing something wrong.

"What are you up to?" John bent down to stroke his friend. He could see why Alfie had been barking with excitement. A hole in the stone facing of the wall had revealed an empty space.

Gently, pulling a piece of the wall away until it was big enough to peer inside, his torch shone on a parcel of some sort. Immediately, John realised this partition had been deliberately put up to hide something. He had two choices: either smash the partition down or open the hole so he could pull out the package. A few minutes later, the gap was big enough to see inside. Much to his surprise, he could see a heavily wrapped item, which he dragged out. Pulling the material away, he found something unbelievable. It was a gold sword covered in precious gemstones.

"Oh my god, what have you found, Alfie?" He moved closer to get a better look with his torch. He couldn't believe it. The sword was beautiful beyond words. My goodness, it must be worth a fortune, but what is it doing hidden away in a wine cellar? He soon discovered that another ledger with handwritten notes dating back to 1944 was hidden in the wall with the artwork. They carefully listed the names of artists and a description of paintings and artefacts. It also listed dates when the stolen artwork had arrived in the villa and when they were shipped out. John was astounded to read they were sent to an address in Austria. He discovered paperwork with the Nazi crest and signatures from senior members of Hitler's henchmen. *'Oh no, this can't be true. It looks like the villa has been used to hide and move stolen works of art.'* He remembered reading about Adolf Hitler's mission to steal priceless paintings during the Second World War. Work had begun in Austria on a magnificent art gallery to house the stolen treasures. It was big business for the Germans to pillage rich villas and galleries and send the items to Austria. The scale of the theft had been enormous, and Italy must have been a heaven-sent gift for the Nazis, being home to so many famous works of art.

Someone had deliberately hidden this sacred sword, but who? Surely Martha's father could not be involved in this deception? Then John realised the magnitude of what he had found. What on earth was he going to do with it? Taking out his phone, he photographed the sword, hoping to research it and find out if it was a copy or an original piece that had disappeared.

He carefully placed the books and sword back inside the wall and filled it up again. With the desk back in place there were no signs of a disturbance. He sat for a moment, trying to take in the enormity of his discovery and the problem of what to do next.

Gone Fishing

(Andato a Pescare)

Italy had been covered in an invisible web of despair. It was struck down by a deathly silence that stretched from the north down to the tip of the toe. The streets, generally filled with music and laughter, had become a dystopian state where no one was allowed out onto the streets unless they had permission from the authorities.

Franco was classed as an essential worker and was able to fish. Mary was determined that Franco was not going out on his boat alone.

"I'm coming with you, Franco. Don't try and stop me."

He laughed when he saw her standing by the boat. She was wearing his old fishing pants and a jacket, and his heart skipped a beat. She looked so sexy.

"All right, you can come, but you must wear this life jacket and follow all my instructions."

"Aye, aye, Captain." She answered.

Half an hour later, the nets had been cast into the water, and now it was a waiting game. Would the fish bite? Or had some mysterious virus struck them also?

Franco, his arm around his wife, hugged her to him. Deep down, he feared that something might happen to her and he would be alone again. He couldn't bear the thought. Mary was everything to him. She immediately quelled his anxiety with her positive attitude and refusal to be defeated.

"Franco, when I married you, I didn't think I would literally become a fisherman's wife," she said as she tried to bring some humour into the situation.

"It was my plan all along, my darling." He replied. "I love you so much I couldn't bear to be separated from you, not even for a minute. Anyway, this is fun, isn't it? You and me all alone out here on the sea." He hugged her closer to him. "Look how beautiful the night is? How many stars are shining down upon us."

Mary glanced up to the sky. A full moon cascaded down on them, sending ripples of silver streaks across the still water, turning the sea from black to violet colour.

"It is so beautiful. Even in these horrible times, it takes your breath away."

Franco himself, captivated by the sight before him, suddenly started to howl like a wild animal.

Mary moved away. 'What on earth are you doing?"

"I'm communicating with nature. We are looking at a wolf moon. In certain countries, the wolf would howl during the cold winter nights to communicate with their pack and to protect their territory. I read that the wolf moon offers a great opportunity for deep self-reflection. And that is what I am doing."

Mary laughed and then joined in, and the sound eerily echoed out into the night and to the horizon.

"Franco, this is crazy, but I have to say I feel better."

"Of course you do. You are communicating with nature."

They stayed together, holding each other close for a while, silently taking in the beautiful scene before them. Eventually, Franco moved towards the edge of the boat and the fishing nets.

"It is time, Maria, to see if we have some fish to feed our customers. Stand back, and I'll winch in the net." He was delighted to see a good selection of squid, sea bass, small swordfish, branzino, crab, and small tuna. "The wolf moon has communicated with the fish. I didn't expect such a big catch." Franco yelled as he emptied the squirming collection over the deck."

"What can I do to help?" Mary said as she tentatively took a step backward.

He looked at her and laughed. She was standing with her arms outstretched to receive the fish. Her eyes closed, and her face screwed up in horror at the anticipation of having to touch them.

"You don't like fish, do you?" he asked gently.

"I love eating them but don't normally get close to them when they are still wriggling around. Look at the poor things. They don't look happy."

Franco laughed. "We could put them back if you want. I could stop fishing, and we could become vegetarians and eat lettuce."

"I wouldn't go that far, Franco. But, look, I'll get the boxes, and you do what you must do. Have we enough, do you think?"

"It's a good catch, Maria. I think we can head home soon."

"Well, I think I could get really good at this. I just need a bit of practice. Would you like me to accompany you again tonight, my darling?"

Franco moved closer to her. He forgot he was holding a baby squid. He reached out to kiss her.

"Oh no, you don't," she squealed as the poor creature jumped out of his hands and slid down her jacket.

Seeking Comfort

(In Cerca di Conforto)

The days dragged slowly by. Although a new routine had been set up, everyone missed the tourists and the excitement of welcoming visitors coming for their summer holidays to experience the fantastic scenery and hospitality this area was famous for. The streets of Sorrento were deserted. No one was allowed out without authorisation. The once busy cobbled pathways were silent, and the shops boarded up, blocking out the sun and any virus lurking in the shadows. What the people were feeling inside their apartments was unknown. They kept a reasonable distance from their neighbours, and the usual sounds of laughter were replaced by the haunting noise of dogs barking and crying out for attention and love.

Signor Miccio had settled into The Villa and felt part of the 'family.' He had almost cried with relief when Martha had invited him to stay. When he heard about the Covid virus, his heart sank.

Anxiety, an emotion that was unknown to him, hit him hard. He thrived on flirting with beautiful ladies. If he had not been born into the hospitality industry, he would have undoubtedly been a flamboyant actor or opera singer performing Puccini's operas on the world's stage.

He was chatting with Eva in the kitchen.

"Dimmi signorina," (tell me, young lady) how are you coping with the quietness?

"I'm struggling," she replied. "I feel frustrated that I can't switch the ovens on and cook for a hundred people. I want to open all the doors and windows and invite everyone in." Eva pummelled the bread she was kneading. It helped to relieve the tension that had been building within her since COVID-19 happened.

"Si, I know how you feel. It is the silence that I am struggling with, also. I have never experienced it before. Sorrento is always full of life and noise. The Signora said to me this morning, 'just listen to the birds singing. Isn't it wonderful? How empty the sky is. No airplanes. It is quite magical.' But, signorina, I find it all very depressing. It has made me feel even more lonely."

She wiped her hands and went towards him.

"I think you need a big hug, Signor. If you would like, you can help me make bread, and we can sing together."

A tear pricked his eyes. This simple act of kindness touched him greatly.

"Si, signorina, let us sing and make bread together."

Within a few moments, as the sunlight streamed through the open doors, the sound of two frightened people began to sing 'O Sole Mio' (my sunshine).' The sound echoed through The Villa, and within minutes, a loud barking could be heard as Alfie crashed through the door to join in.

"Trust him to smell the food," Eva laughed. "Come here, you little mongrel." She picked him up and held him close. Meanwhile, Signor Miccio had progressed his repertoire with a rendition of 'Torna a Surriento.' Eva and Alfie, their eyes wide open, were mesmerised by the power of the voice of this little round man. The joy of music had brought them together; sunshine and hope literally invaded the room.

Lorenzo

(Lorenzo)

The daily death toll in Italy was rising dramatically, and the hospital was still inundated with casualties.

Sam collapsed into a chair, allowing the tears to flow to release the tension building up within her all day. Exhaustion was a permanent feature. How much longer will this go on? Already, it was the third month of this dreadful virus. The only hope on the horizon was news about a vaccine. It had to work. Otherwise, the deaths would just continue daily.

She sighed as she wiped her eyes and put on a clean mask. *'I had better get back to my patients. Now is not the time to feel sorry for myself. There is so much work to do.'*

A voice behind her called her name.

"Samantha, posso avere una parola?" (Can I have a word?)

She turned to face a senior doctor. "Si, of course."

"It is about Dr Rossi. He has been taken into intensive care."

"Oh my god! Does he have Covid?"

"Yes, it was in the early hours when he suddenly had difficulty breathing. It came on so quickly. Fortunately, he was in the right place and has been intubated. I'm afraid he is very ill."

'Can I see him?" Samantha was trying hard not to cry. Lorenzo meant so much to her

"Yes, come with me. I'm sure your presence will help him."

Samantha was horrified with what faced her. Poor Lorenzo was unconscious and hooked to machines. His face was ashen, and he was totally unaware of her presence. She searched for any signs of life. Youth and time were on his side. The care and treatment he was receiving in the hospital could not have been better, but she was aware that he was exhausted, and worried his body might not have the strength to fight off the virus. It was impossible to say. She had witnessed some people recover, and others did not.

After an hour of sitting quietly next to him, she reluctantly had to return to care for the patients on her ward.

The days drifted into nights, and as soon as Sam had finished her shift, she went to sit with Lorenzo; only moving to help the doctors and nurses turn him over. The hours passed by, and his condition deteriorated. It was a struggle for Sam to stay awake, and at times, she found herself sleeping next to him. At one point, she had held his hand and whispered gently to him, his face strangely peaceful as he hovered between this world and the next.

"You are not alone," she said. "I'm here for you, my darling. I will always be by your side." She stared into the face of the young man who had meant so much to her. They had a future together, but it wasn't meant to be.

"Has he gone?" the doctor asked as he stood beside her. Samantha looked at Lorenzo lying in bed. A cold shiver swept through her. In her mind, she had been staring into Robbie's face, not Lorenzo.

"No, he's clinging on. It's touch and go. I wish I could do something."

"You are Samantha. You are by his side. Lorenzo has a lot to live for. His body may be able to overcome the virus. You must have hope."

"Yes, of course,"

This was too much to bear. All the memories of her beautiful husband had come flooding back as she had held his hand, and he, too, had slipped away from the ravages of cancer. Now, her dear friend, who had helped her to overcome her grief, was in the same place. She couldn't let him die.

"Come on, Lorenzo, we need you ... I need you. Keep fighting, please. I can't go through this again."

John's Secret

(Il Segreto di Giovanni)

The Bay of Naples had taken on a golden glow as the slow-moving sun spread a celebratory shower of tangerine and lemon colour to end the daylight hours.

Mary and Franco were lying side by side in their lugger boat. A woollen blanket helped to protect them from the cool air.

"Look at the sky, Franco. It is just awesome."

"If only we could capture this moment forever. It is how the world should be calm and peaceful." He held Mary's hand. "It has been such a wonderful day. I am the luckiest man in the world." He turned and gently kissed her.

Mary responded by snuggling closer to him and closing her eyes as they drifted off to sleep.

Two hours later, they awoke to darkness and a magical sky full of stars shining down on them.

"Oh my goodness, Franco, wake up. We drifted off to sleep."

Stretching slightly to ease the crick in his neck, he laughed at her.

"Good job, I anchored. We would have been in the middle of the ocean by now."

"We had better head home. It's getting late."

A short time later, they were staring into the almost empty fridge in the kitchen.

"Such a shame you are such a bad fisherman, Franco. We didn't catch anything."

"It wasn't my fault. Besides, it is my day off, and you kept distracting me."

"Me! I was too busy listening to you saying we would catch a big fish, take it home, and cook it together over the open fire."

"Yes, I remember saying that, but with the calm sea and my new wife by my side, I forgot all about the fish. Anyway, I'm hungry, woman. What are you cooking me?"

"Franco, my darling, I will cook your favourite meal. A Spanish omelette!"

Franco quickly took out his phone. "I'll just ring Eva and see what food she has in the fridge."

"Don't you dare? You are having a Spanish

omelette."

"It sounds perfetta. Can I do anything?"

"Yes, chop the veg. I'll open the wine."

Just as they had started to prepare their supper, they heard the sound of footsteps running up the wooden stairs from outside.

"I wonder who this is?" Franco said as he put on his facemask before he opened the door.

"John, come in. What brings you here at this time of night."

"Hi guys, I'm so sorry to disturb you. I hope you don't mind me calling in."

"Not at all, John. Is everything all right? You look a bit stressed." Mary said as she pulled a wooden chair nearer to him. "We are just about to have some food. Would you like to join us?"

"No, no, thank you. I won't keep you long. I shouldn't be here, but I need to talk to you. I have a problem, and I don't know what to do. I need your advice."

"Of course, we will be happy to help. What's happened?"

"Well, I decided to clear the wine cellar. Martha

and I thought we could put it to some use as a place for guests to sit and have a drink and nibbles. It's great inside, with lovely stone walls and vaulted ceilings. We can do a lot with it. Anyway, Martha showed me another room filled with old bottles of her father's wine. It was also the room he used as an office. Martha was busy, so Alfie and I were happy to clean up.' He paused for a moment to catch his breath. "I was really enjoying it. Alberto, her father, had all his ledgers for the wine production in his desk drawer. It's exciting."

Mary looked at Franco, wondering where this conversation was heading.

"Then Alfie started digging furiously at a crack in the wall. I tried to pull him away, but I noticed it was a false wall. I pulled down the stone and, well, I couldn't believe what I saw."

"What, John, what was it?" Mary leaned closer to him.

"This," he said.

Mary took the phone from him. She could see a glittering mass of jewels set in an ancient sword. She passed the phone to Franco.

"I didn't understand at first, but then I found a hidden ledger. It was full of entries and descriptions of works of art stored in the wine cellar, and guess what? It was dated 1945. They were stolen priceless masterpieces, and next to each entry was the initial AR. It gave details of where they were shipped to, and also the paper it was written on had the Nazi symbol."

Franco stared at John. "Mamma Mia, John. I'm no expert, but this looks very precious. Look how beautiful it is. My God, this is serious. I remember hearing stories about how the Germans stole priceless paintings and artefacts from galleries and private houses. Hitler was building his own museum in Austria, and the items were moved there."

"I don't understand." Mary interrupted. "Are you saying The Villa was the base to store these works of art?"

"It does point to that, Mary," John said. "The AR signature is Alberto Russo, Martha's father."

"Oh my God. Do you think she knows about it?

Should we tell her?" Mary asked.

"We must tell the Police, as this sword should be returned to its rightful owner. We could be in serious trouble if we don't." John replied

"No, no, we can't do that, John. Martha would be devastated. All her memories of her father would be destroyed. I think it would kill her."

"I agree. Martha must never know." Franco said.

"Of course, you are right. I just needed someone to confirm that to me. For the time being, the wall is temporarily sealed. Thanks, guys. I had to tell somebody. I don't like secrets, but Martha needs to be protected from this."

"John, pull up a chair and eat with us," Franco suggested.

"Yes, it looks like you've had quite a day." Mary agreed.

"Yes, I think I will," John said as he accepted a glass of red wine. "We should think about what to do. Goodness, who would have thought we have a priceless work of art on our hands."

"Well, at least it's safe where it is," Mary said,

and then she decided to change the subject. "Have you heard from Samantha? We have been thinking about her, especially after hearing the news tonight. It's very worrying. The virus seems to be getting worse everywhere, especially where Sam and Lorenzo are."

"No, we haven't. Martha is getting anxious as she keeps asking me what's happening. It could be a long time before The Villa opens again for visitors."

"It's so scary," Mary said as she placed the supper dishes on the table. "I guess we are all in the same situation. I just can't believe what is happening. We hadn't even met this time last year, let alone started a business." She looked at Franco. "And you and I were just memories from years ago, and look at us now. We are married and confined to spending twenty-four hours a day together." She laughed. "Who would have thought?"

"Mia cara moglie, (my darling wife). Are you complaining? I can always disappear to my boat."

Mary leaned over the table and blew him a

kiss. "Amo ogni momento passato con te. (I love every moment spent with you)."

John stared at the two people in front of him. They meant the world to him. A short while later, he and Alfie said goodbye and started their long, lonely walk back up the road to The Villa, happy he had confided in people he could trust. He felt he would sleep well tonight.

Lockdown Ends

(Il Blocco Termina)

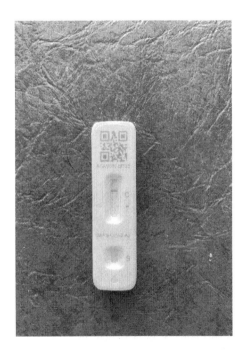

The news that Lockdown was to end was a huge relief to everyone. John was a man who needed to be busy. He put his heart and soul into breathing life back into the vineyard. All the comments from the local wine producers had been positive, and he had acted on their advice and restocked with new vines when the old ones had become weary and tired.

"Ciao, John. Do you need any help?" Franco was heading in his direction.

'Ciao, Franco, I always need an extra pair of hands. I'm just trimming the vines and whispering words of love to them so they produce a good healthy crop for me."

Franco laughed. "Here, let me help." He picked up a pair of secateurs and carefully cut away the dead wood.

"You've done this before."

"Of course, we Italians are very talented in every aspect of life."

They worked quietly for a while, concentrating on the delicate work.

"The vines are looking very good, John. I think you may get a good crop this year."

"I hope so. I've got the wine cellar all cleaned out and ready for the day we start producing our own wine."

"I don't think I've seen the cellar," Franco said. "Maybe you could show me?"

"Yes, let's take a break. Come on, tell me what you think."

Ten minutes later, John proudly opened the heavy wooden door and waited for Franco's reaction.

"Mamma Mia," he exclaimed. "My God, this is amazing." Franco walked around the brightly lit cellar. You've done a great job. I love the original stonework, and the arched domes are beautiful."

"Martha and I thought it would make an added attraction to the restaurant if we opened it up to the public. I've put some twinkling white lights in. Here, let me show you." John switched on the display of lights. We are trying to create an ambiance while keeping it traditional with the original wine barrels. Maybe we will do a wine-tasting evening with cheese, nibbles, or even intimate wedding ceremonies. What do you think?"

"It sounds like it could be a success, John, especially if you bottle your vintage. Maybe display and sell your olive oil in a small shop area. We could get Eva and Henrik to make some limoncello. The tourists love it. Franco looked around. "Where does this lead to?" He asked, pointing to the office door.

"It's the office Martha's father used. Come, I'll show you. This is the room I told you about where I found the sword. Look, this is his desk containing his records of wine production. It's quite interesting." John reached for a bottle of wine off the oak shelving. "This is The Villa's label. What do you think?"

"I like it. Are you going to use it?"

"I'm not sure. I think I'll get Enzo, the artist who did a good job on the bedrooms, to create something similar but more up-to-date."

"Good idea, John." Franco looked around the room. "It's quite dark in here compared to the cellar. There is a historical feel to this room. You can almost see Martha's father sitting in the chair."

"It's the first time I've been in here since I told you and Mary about the sword."

"Where is it? Can I see it?"

John went to lock the office door so they wouldn't be interrupted, and then he moved the desk and chair to one side to reveal the stonewall.

"It's in here." He said as he started to pull away at the stones to reveal the secret hiding place. He gently pulled out the sword, which was wrapped in protective material.

"What do you make of this?" he said as he revealed the ancient relic.

Franco was taken aback. He immediately crossed himself as though in the presence of a holy spirit.

"My God, It must be worth a fortune."

"Certainly the gems are real and the actual sword, I think, is gold. These are the records the

Germans kept."

John pulled out the ledgers and laid them on the desk.

"These are accounts of the stolen items stored here during the Second World War. Strangely, I can't find any record of this particular piece."

"It's unbelievable. I know this sort of thing went on, but discovering evidence of it is quite remarkable." Franco said.

John nodded. "I've been thinking about it. It's been here so long. Maybe we should leave it where it is, and eventually, and I'm not testing fate here, but when Martha passes away, maybe we can reveal what we have found."

"For now, I think that is the best thing to do. Here, John, let me help you put it back in the wall. I don't think anyone would find it."

Martha's Confession

(La Confessione di Marta)

A month later, Franco was again helping John cultivate the grape vines. The spring had brought hot weather, and they paused to take a break.

"I didn't realize how much effort was put into producing a glass of wine." John sank to the ground. He had been working hard since sunrise, and the heat was beginning to get to him.

"Ah, John, the most pleasurable things in life need the most strenuous effort to create. Perfection is a work of art. Enticing someone to fall in love with you takes patience and mystery. But the outcome is worth it. Take the sword, for example. It just didn't happen. Men would have been made to work in the mines, risking their lives, to hew out these jewels. They would probably have been badly treated, and the craftsman who made the finished article would also have been at the mercy of his master."

"Yes, you are right. I have been worrying about the sword and what to do with it. I think we should tell Martha. She has a right to know."

"Sono d'accordo, John (I agree)."

Franco was unaware Martha was walking towards them and had overheard their conversation.

"Tell Martha what?" Franco turned around to face her. "What is the problem, John? I think you should tell me." She looked directly at him.

John sighed. It would appear that the moment had arrived.

"Shall we sit down? Franco and I have discovered something in the wine cellar. We didn't want to tell you, but it is very serious and could affect The Villa."

Martha moved to a nearby bench in the shade. She took out her fan to cool herself and prepare for what would come.

"OK, I'm ready. Dimmi caro (tell me, dear)."

"Do you remember when we decided to clean out the wine cellar? I was delighted to find all the paperwork in your father's office regarding the wine harvests going back over time." John glanced at Franco, who was listening intently. "He had recorded everything meticulously, and it was really helpful. Then Alfie started scratching the wall, and after investigating, I realised it was a false section. I managed to rip part of it away, and then I couldn't believe my eyes. I saw an object. It was a jewelled sword and was wrapped carefully in a blanket. I also found some ledgers dating back to 1943. They contained records of stolen artwork that had been stored in the cellar by the Nazis."

He could tell Martha was listening carefully, but her expression didn't give anything away.

"The records had the German crest and a signature against the lists. It was your father's signature. It appears that he was involved in the embezzlement of priceless artworks."

"I see, John. Well, I presume you wish to protect me from this discovery." She looked at each of them and said. "The truth is I have always known what was going off. I was nearly ten years old in 1943, and I remember very clearly the

German occupation of Italy. My father worked hard on the land, and my grandfather, who built this villa, also worked tirelessly to create the vineyard and everything we see today.

During this time, the Germans were billeted in the monastery nearby. The liberators were making headway from the north and south. Although we were unaware of that, we were told the Germans were winning the war. Italy was about to join the battles on the other side and become part of the Allied forces. Mussolini's days were numbered. Everything was changing."

John and Franco listened, intrigued, as Martha continued with her memories.

"I was a curious child, quite grown up for my years, and when I heard noises deep in the night, I would look out of my bedroom window, and I saw things. I was careful not to be seen, but one day, the German Capitan turned up, and my father took him to his office. I was sent indoors, but as soon as possible, I followed and hid behind the wine barrels in the cellar. The German explained that the army had orders to evacuate and head north. He said there wasn't time to take the sword, and he wanted my father to hide it and that he would return for it after the war. He threatened to kill the entire family if it wasn't here when he returned."

Martha paused for a moment. Then, the memories came flooding back to her.

"I remember thinking, please don't kill Papa. How would we survive without him? But my father was calm and agreed to hide the sword until he returned."

"Goodness, Martha, that must have been a terrifying moment for you," John said.

"I didn't quite understand what they were talking about, but life had been frightening for a long time, John. We had become accustomed to the German occupation but didn't like it. My father was wise. To protect his family, he went along with the Nazis. I hated this man. He was powerful and constantly stared at me with cold blue eyes. My father would tell me to go inside out of the way, but the German would tease me, probably because I always glared at him.

"The thing is, Martha, the sword is still hidden away all this time."

Martha glanced down at her hands. She was quiet.

"Yes, John, I know it's there. I decided to protect my father's reputation and not reveal its whereabouts. The problem was that the Germans were clever and paid my father a small amount to store paintings. This incriminated him, and I couldn't risk him being prosecuted for something we, as a family, had no choice in being part of. It was such a frightening time. People were turning against each other. It was terrible. Everyone was scared for their lives."

"How did George react when you told him," John asked.

"I didn't tell him. It was my Papa who explained all about the art fraud to him. George and my father got on so well together. In the evenings, they used to disappear into the wine cellar. In fact, my mother would laugh about it, saying they were up to no good. Then, George and I arrived from London one day for our annual holiday.

George had gone down to the cove for a swim, and I was helping Papa in the garden. We were cutting flowers for the house." Martha frowned as though reliving the memory. "My mamma was ill and confined to bed. Papa was struggling mentally to look after her. After all these years, they were still in love, and Papa couldn't bear to see her in pain. The doctors were optimistic, but I felt they were not telling us the whole story. We knew her health was failing quickly and that Papa would need us. I was just about to say I would stay in Italy to look after them both when a car came up the drive. I was horrified to immediately recognise it was Hoffman. I couldn't believe it, especially after all this time. My father quickly grabbed my arm and told me to go inside the house immediately.

I retaliated and told him I was not going anywhere and that I was not a child and wouldn't leave him alone with that man. I wondered why he had returned, but my father knew why. In fact, he had been waiting for this day to arrive since the war had ended.

My father insisted I go and check on my mother. He didn't want her to know had returned. I reluctantly agreed.

Papa invited him to the wine cellar to taste our new vintage. Sometime later, I clearly heard the sound of a gunshot. I rushed outside to see George running across the courtyard towards the cellar. I followed him, and we saw my father leaning over the Capitan, who was lying on the floor. Blood was oozing out of him. I was horrified. I couldn't accept that my father had killed him. It was like being in the middle of a nightmare. Papa was in shock and wasn't making any sense. George examined the German and confirmed he was dead.

Eventually, my father told us the Nazi had pulled a gun on him and papa was quick to react and in the struggle Herr Hoffman got shot. Papa told us about our home being used to hide stolen artworks during the war, and the Capitan had returned to reclaim a priceless sword my father had been hiding in a secret place. I didn't tell him I already knew about it. I didn't want him to know I had eavesdropped as a child."

Franco leaned over to touch Martha on her arm to comfort her.

"Are you sure you want to continue, Martha? We didn't mean to upset you."

"I'm not upset, Franco. In a way, it is a relief to get it all out in the open. My father was not to blame for any of it. We were just victims of the war. We have been lucky. No one in the family was killed. We didn't lose our property; we just had to do as we were told; otherwise, we would have been killed. Everyone was in fear. My country was in pain, and we were only ordinary country people." She paused a moment to take a breath. "I am sure you are wondering what happened next?"

"Only if you want to tell us, Martha," John spoke quietly.

"Well, we had a body to dispose of? There was blood everywhere. George instinctively took over the situation, as my father was distressed.

He suggested we wrap the German in old sacks and find somewhere to bury him later that night when it was dark. It was my father who suggested we take him to the monastery graveyard. The monks would be asleep. It sounded like the best option.

I gave my Papa a drink of brandy, and we assured him everything would be OK. We told him that George and I would dispose of the body, but he insisted on coming with us, saying that the Nazi had haunted him most of his life and he needed to see with his own eyes that he was buried. Martha paused. "And that is what happened all those years ago."

"But the monastery. Did the monks know?" John said.

"No, of course not. We dragged Hoffman to an area near the trees. My father and George dug a deep grave, and we buried him. To this day, no one has come looking for him."

"It is an amazing story, Martha. You should write a book about your experiences. You need to share it with the world."

"Maybe, John, when I have gone on to join dear George and my family, I could leave my memoirs for posterity. Then, the sword could be placed in a cathedral and be seen by the whole world again. Anyway, for now, we will keep it hidden in the wall."

"Franco and I will make sure it stays there. Let us walk you back to The Villa." John said kindly as he took the old lady's arm.

Homecoming
(Ritorno a Casa)

It had been three long months, and the virus was finally slowing down. The lockdown had brought many challenges to the Italian people, many of whom lived in blocks of apartments with little outside space. Only the small balconies brought people out to take in the fresh air, and an amazing thing soon started to happen. Singing became the norm. Operatic voices could be heard in the warm night air, and shouting to neighbours was a heartwarming nightly occurrence. Solo violinist saw the opportunity to delight friends with classical wizardry, and romantic attachments were formed across the balconies. Romeo and Juliet had been reborn.

The Villa was buzzing with excitement. The possibility of opening the restaurant for a few hours was enough to send everyone into frenzy. Tables were moved to keep a reasonable distance between diners while trying to keep an intimate atmosphere.

The good news was the possibility of a vaccine becoming available soon. Suddenly, everyone's spirits were lifted. Even though foreign travel was still restricted for all countries, hope was on the horizon. For a short time, it looked very optimistic.

The kitchen was in full preparation. Henrik and Eva had decided on a tapas/antipasto event rather than a full-scale opening. Food supplies were limited, so offering small portions of delicious tasting crab ravioli, olives, slices of pizza, a variety of small pasta dishes, and fresh crispy salad from the garden made sense. Cheese and fruit were added so people could choose finger foods. Of course, Eva and Henrik went to town on homemade sausage rolls and tiny pasties. For dessert, some colourful, fresh, tangy sorbets, an enormous Zabaglione with fresh fruits, and a Pasterera Napoletana made from ricotta cheese, candied peel, and orange flower water.

Signor Miccio was already singing as he went around the restaurant, checking and double-checking that the tables had beautiful garden flowers and the best crystal glasses. After all, this would be the special evening everyone had been eagerly waiting for.

A sports car appeared at the entrance to the driveway. It made its way tentatively up the gravelled road, drawing to a stop at the entrance to The Villa.

"Hey everyone, come and look. It's Samantha. She's come home." John shouted as he and Alfie rushed out to greet her.

"John, how wonderful to see you."

"Hi, Samantha, but who is that with you?" he asked. He noticed a figure wrapped in a thin blanket lying horizontally on the back seat.

"It's Lorenzo. Oh, John, he has been so ill, he nearly died. I couldn't leave him behind. Don't worry; he doesn't have Covid anymore, just suffering the after-effects."

"Oh my word, look at you," Martha said as she joined them.

"Samantha darling, you look so tired. Henrik, can you help John get Lorenzo inside?"

"He is frail but can walk a little," Sam said as she stepped out of the car.

Eva headed for a big hug with her arms outstretched, but Samantha pulled back. "It's lovely to see you all, but I'll keep my distance for a while. It's been a long journey, and I must take a test to ensure I'm not bringing anything in. Oh my, it's so good to see you. How are you all?

"We've had it easy compared to everyone else," Eva said.

"Martha, I hope you don't mind me bringing Lorenzo here. At the moment, he is not well enough to look after himself."

"I am so glad you did. We'll soon get his strength back. Come this way. We have a lovely room for him. Of course, you haven't seen what we have done to the bedrooms."

"Thank you, Martha. It's so good to be home. I have missed you all."

Once Lorenzo was settled comfortably into his room, Samantha headed for the kitchen.

"What's happening? It looks like you are reopening?"

"Yes, our first night. We have a few problems with food supplies, so we have gone for a selection of finger foods and lots of wine."

"Are you expecting many people?" Sam asked.

"We've limited it to 30 to make it more comfortable."

Samantha smiled. "It will take a long time before people feel confident and life returns to normal. We may experience a repeat of the virus or even a variation may appear. The world has to heal. But looking around, everything looks so beautiful. I can't wait to be normal again. It's been horrendous."

"Darling Samantha, you are worn out. Why don't you go and have a hot shower and a sleep? We can have a long chat later." Martha said.

"No, I'm alright, Martha, thank you. I'm eager to hear everyone's news. Where are Mary and Franco?"

"Well, you'll never believe what they are doing.

Since the pandemic, they have resurrected the traditional art form of selling fish via baskets to people stuck in apartment buildings. Franco yells, 'Oh pesce,' and the women drop down a basket on a rope with a note and money inside, and Mary sorts the order, and the basket is hauled back up." Martha laughed. "I never thought I would ever see the day when we went back to those methods. Mary even joins Franco when he takes the fishing boat out. She's become an expert at hauling the nets in. He said she's a natural but can't wait to get home and shower to get rid of the smell of fish!"

"Don't you think it's amazing how people have adjusted to a different way of living?" Samantha said. "I think more people would have died if we hadn't gone into lockdown straight away, and with the vaccine on the horizon, it is looking really hopeful."

"I hope so, my dear, I really do."

"Can I get you something to eat?" Eva said as she poured steaming tea into a china cup. "We have some chicken vegetable soup left over from lunch or perhaps some cake?"

"I wouldn't say no to a piece of lemon cake. I've been unable to take my eyes off it since I walked into the kitchen. I'm sure the soup would do Lorenzo good." Sam said.

Eva passed the large lemon sponge over to her.

"I think you will like this. It's made from homegrown lemons, and I've added a touch of our very own limoncello. You should see what John has done to the wine cellar. While waiting for the grapes to be perfect, we have been looking into making our own olive oil, limoncello, and bottled tomato chutney, which we hope to sell from a stall in the wine cellar. We've also been selling cakes and bread from a table set up in Piazza Tasso. It's all been done very carefully. We leave a fresh delivery and an honesty tin, and people pop out and take what they need."

Henrik entered the kitchen and joined in the conversation.

"Our takeaway service is proving so successful that we may not even bother opening the restaurant again."

"He's joking, Sam. I can't keep him out of the kitchen. We all want to be back to our real jobs." Eva laughed as she hugged Henrik. "We have kept busy, and it helped to keep our mind off things."

"I've missed you all so much you wouldn't believe. And I have just realised that I haven't congratulated you on your engagement. It's the best news ever. Let me see the ring."

The small diamond glistened as it caught the afternoon sunlight from the window.

"It's gorgeous. What did Franco say when you told him?"

"Henrik did the man thing and asked him if he had any objections to proposing to me. Can you imagine that? My father was very emotional, and Henrik had to comfort him."

"So, how did he propose?" Sam asked. "Did he get down on one knee?"

"It was the day you left to go up north, and there was snow on Vesuvius, so we drove to Monte Faito for a picnic."

Henrik interrupted. "It was a magical and special moment I will never forget, especially as she said 'yes.' We went into lockdown a few days later, so we haven't had a moment to plan or celebrate."

"Well, as soon as things settle, we'll have a big party. I've really missed this place so much. But good times will come back." Samantha took another slice of cake. "Eva, this is delicious; I missed your cooking."

"Samantha, Lorenzo is awake and asking for you," John said as he entered the room. "I'm just getting him a drink. He doesn't want any food yet."

"I'll take it, John. How did he seem to you?"

"I think he was surprised to see me. He vaguely remembers arriving, but I can tell he is absolutely worn out."

"Oh John, it was touch and go whether he would survive. At one point, the machines were keeping him alive. But now we have hope that he will improve."

"Well, we have abundant love, not to mention good food, and we will do our best to get him well."

Samantha headed upstairs with a jug of fresh fruit juice in her hand. Alfie was lying protectively on the bed beside Lorenzo, drifting in and out of sleep.

"How are you feeling?" she gently asked him.

"Just tired, Sam, but so glad to be here."

"I'm pleased to have got you back safely. The traffic was a nightmare. I have no intention of ever driving through Rome or Naples again." She laughed. "Everyone is eager to get you on your feet as soon as possible, so all you need to do is follow orders and rest."

Lorenzo gently took her hand. "Sam, I am so sorry for dragging you to Bergamo." He coughed uncontrollably, and she quickly passed a glass of water to him.

"Hush, there is no need to say anything. I wanted to help, and I don't regret a thing. I'm just sorry you have been so ill. But I'm going to make sure you get better."

He squeezed her hand. "I'm so lucky," he started to say and closed his eyes.

"There now, get some sleep. Alfie is next to you to keep you company. I'm sure he will bark if you wake up."

Sam sat for a few moments. She stared at Lorenzo. Unlike most Italian men, his normal complexion was pale owing to having so little time to spend in the sunshine. Tears came into her eyes. He looked so vulnerable. Usually, he had a healthy look, but now it was very apparent that he had been seriously ill. His strong face appeared shrunken. She knew her emotions were very close to the surface. It didn't seem that long ago that she had been staring into her husband's eyes, Robbie, willing him to fight his cancer. Now Sam was in a similar situation with a man she cared for and felt she could one day love like she had with Robbie.

Samantha didn't hear the door open as Mary entered the room, and seeing the look on Sam's face, she threw her arms around her and gently hugged her.

'Poor Lorenzo, he looks so poorly. We will have

to work hard to get him better again, but I'm sure he will pick up now he can rest."

Samantha smiled, "this is just what he needs: a lot of people fussing and looking after him. How are you, Mary? I've missed you."

"I'm good. Franco and I are keeping busy. We will all be glad when we can get back to normal again."

"I hear you have taken up fishing?" Samantha laughed.

"Believe me, its not through choice. I can't stand the smell of fish. In fact, I don't like it when they are wriggling at the bottom of the boat. They look so miserable. I want to throw them back in the water. The great thing is that Franco and I are out there on the sea at night watching the stars. I love that part. When Lorenzo feels better, you should both join us. It is wonderful to be so close to nature."

"It's a date."

Mary looked at Samantha carefully. "I know you have been through a nightmare, but are you alright? You look a bit peeky."

Tears again formed in Sam's eyes.

"I'm five months pregnant." She said simply.

"Oh my God, Samantha. I had no idea.

"Baggy clothes help." Sam smiled.

'How do you feel about that?" Mary said.

Sam turned to look at Lorenzo to make sure he was sleeping. "I honestly don't know. It happened at Christmas. We were beginning to get close. Lorenzo is such a lovely guy, and he was so kind to me. I think I was feeling a bit vulnerable. You know Christmas can be lonely when you have lost someone you love. We just came together, two lonely people. It was really special, and I was taken by surprise. Afterward, I felt confused and guilty. I love Robbie, but he's gone, and I know I'll never see him again. Lorenzo was there, full of life and kindness. Yes, it was that simple act of someone loving me, and now, as if proof of that moment, I'm having his baby."

"Does he know Sam?"

"No, Mary, there was no time in Bergamo. I hardly saw him. We spent most of the time in the hospital. In fact, I only realised about two months ago. I'd been feeling sick and so exhausted I thought I had Covid, but it wasn't. I'm a nurse, yet I couldn't even diagnose my own symptoms."

"If you don't mind me saying, it is wonderful news, a new life coming into your world just when you need and deserve it. Don't worry about the practical side of things. We will all be here to help you and Lorenzo. Why don't you go and have a rest and then come and join us in the restaurant later? I'll sit with Lorenzo for a while."

"Thanks, Mary, I think I will. I am feeling tired after that long drive. It must be all the excitement of coming home."

Samantha didn't manage the opening evening in the restaurant. She opened her bedroom door and was relieved that she had returned home and everything would be all right. Lorenzo was relaxed, and he, too, could start to recuperate from his illness. Samantha quickly unpacked her bag and placed the photograph of Robbie by her bedside table. His smiling face stared at her, and for a moment, she felt she had let him down. She lay on the bed and let her thoughts drift back to her marriage to Robbie. It was so wonderful. His happy, kind disposition, love of life, and fun captured her heart from the first moment she met him. After their romantic wedding in the Cloisters in Sorrento, their future was so bright. Samantha clutched the photograph to her heart.

'I will always love you, my darling, and I will never forget you. You would want me to move on. I didn't plan for this to happen, but it has, and I'm having his baby. He is a good man; I know you would have liked him. I'm confused and probably still grieving. My emotions are all over the place. But I'm back in The Villa with people who love and will help me. So please don't worry.'

She climbed into bed. The constant noise of ambulance and police sirens were back in Bergamo. Now, all she could hear was the gentle buzz of home, which helped her to drift into a deep sleep as soon as she put her head on the pillow.

***

Two days later, Lorenzo felt well enough to sit outside on the terrace. He was watching Samantha, who was laughing with Mary. They were trying to pick lemons off the trees for another batch of limoncello. He could see the shape of her body starting to change. It had been a shock this morning when she told him she was pregnant with his child. He immediately felt guilty for putting her in this position. Goodness, guilt was firmly implanted in his head. All the patients he had been unable to save with Covid. Their suffering was etched in his brain. He could quite literally sit and cry for their lost lives. Now, the woman he admired for her strength and kindness was having his baby, a child he never dreamt he would have. He had to hold back the tears as overwhelming joy swept over him.

He remembered quite vividly the night they spent together at Christmas. She filled his heart with happiness. Something he had not felt for a long time. They danced in the moonlight. Serendipity played its part when the magic came together. Enchantment echoed through the music, the soft light, and the view of Sorrento Bay glittering like tiny fireflies that kissed and danced in the air together. Her laughing face mesmerized him. All the hurt she had endured with the loss of the love of her life fleetingly vanished. For one moment, she was his, and she wanted him. And now she was pregnant, and he had no idea how she felt about having his child. Was it his imagination that she didn't mention love? Did she love him? Or was it a rebound effect from Robbie's death??

Lorenzo had a charmed upbringing. His parents were wealthy Neapolitan business people. Everything in life was given to him. He only had to ask. But the only thing he desired was love. To feel the exhilaration of loving another person and being totally loved in return. He had experienced a lot of women. Many would have married him instantly, but his career as a doctor was the most important thing to him. Then Samantha walked into his life, and he was shot in the heart by Cupid's arrow.

Having Covid had frightened him. He had always been fit and strong, but now, even the slightest effort left him feeling washed out and fragile. And this added news that Samantha was very much pregnant had come as a complete surprise. Secretly, he was delighted, although he wasn't sure how she felt about it. One of the things that attracted him to her was her strength of character and ability to adapt to any situation. He knew her feelings for Robbie were still very strong, but he felt, with time, maybe she could look forward to a good life with him and their child. He wanted it, but he had decided to wait and give them time to recover. He sighed and closed his eyes as the warm sunlight drifted across his face. If only he could get rid of this awful feeling of fatigue. He desperately wanted to be fit and strong again. Closing his eyes and taking a few deep breaths to calm his anxiety, his body swept him back into a deep sleep. Sam glanced over to check on him. She could see he was asleep again. Poor Lorenzo, he had been through so much.

Mary leaned over to Samantha.

"Have you told him yet?"

"Yes, this morning."

"How did he take it?" Mary asked bluntly

"Poor Lorenzo, he has so much going off in his head now. I think to learn he will be a father must have really shocked him."

"Of course, it must have done, but Sam, what did he say to you?"

"Well, he said he was delighted at the news but wouldn't pressure me into any kind of commitment, although he would provide for and be here for me and the baby. He suggested we just take time and take each day as it comes. And then he hugged me, and I realised he was crying."

"An honourable man. Personally, I think that is a wonderful reaction and very sensible. I know he cares for you. I've seen how he looks at you when you are not looking."

"I care for him too, Mary, but I am so confused. One minute, I saw Robbie lying in the hospital bed, and the next, I was holding Lorenzo's hand and praying he didn't die."

"I think you have feelings for him but need more

time. Have you told your parents yet?"

"I'm going to ring them this evening. I don't know what they will say. I'd better tell everyone here, although I'm not looking forward to it."

"Don't be silly. They will all be delighted for you both. You don't have to explain too much. It's your business. I think they will understand and will be there to support all three of you. Besides, you are five months pregnant, and no matter how you hide your shape, your baby wants to make itself known to the world." Mary smiled. "Imagine Martha's reaction. She will be the perfect nonna. As for John, I can see him now pushing the pram down to the vineyard. Your child will grow up with such love and become an expert in cooking, treading grapes, and fishing, not to mention singing. Gosh, so many things." They laughed together. "Come on, we had better get these lemons inside and crack on with the limoncello."

They headed to the kitchen and checked on Lorenzo, who was sleeping peacefully.

"That's what he needs," Mary said, "sunshine and

calm. He'll soon be back to his normal self."

Samantha smiled. "Yes, that is exactly what will make him well again. I'll get him a cold drink. I need to keep him hydrated."

Mary smiled. Little escaped her notice where romance was concerned. She had felt from the moment they met that they were right for each other. They just needed a little outside help and what could be better than a baby.

Samantha carried a jug of lemonade and two glasses over to Lorenzo. He was awake and moved over to let her sit beside him.

"Hey, lazy bones, what are you doing in the sunshine?"

She smiled at him, and suddenly, he became alive again at the sight of her.

"I'm following your orders, Signora."

"Good. I will get you back to full strength if it's the last thing I do."

"Do you want to come in the kitchen and help Mary and I prepare all the gorgeous lemons we've picked?"

"In a little while, I'm just so comfortable here with Alfie looking after me."

She bent to kiss him on his cheek and was taken aback by the strange look in his eyes.

"You are feeling OK, aren't you?" she asked.

"I am so much better. You mustn't worry about me. I've enjoyed watching you laughing with Mary. It feels like life is getting back to normal."

"Lorenzo, it will, and you will soon be better. We just need time to adjust. It's been a shock to everyone, but it is nearly over. Oh, goodness. The baby just kicked me. He must be agreeing with me."

"Can I feel?"

"Of course." She placed his hand over her stomach, and together they marvelled as their baby, obviously just waking up, moved inside her.

"How do you know it's a boy?" he asked.

"I don't. I just have a feeling. What do you think?"

"I think it's a boy too. Trust me, I know about these things. I'm a doctor."

***

Samantha's News
(Le Novita di Samantha)

Although life was far from normal, The Villa slipped into a different existence. Eva had calmed down, and she and Henrik were immersed in their website and podcasts. Their followers had reached over 500,000, and interest in The Villa and the restaurant showed an increase in bookings for the following year.

Coronavirus hadn't gone away. Tourists were still locked in their own world, googling exotic places and dreaming of getting back on a plane again.

Henrik was adding up their first evening takings, after lockdown. "Looks like it was a successful night, guys."

"Si, molto bene," Signor Miccio was delighted. "Although I think the guests come to see me and not to eat the food."

"Don't let Eva hear you say that." Henrik slapped him on his back, "But I think you have a point. Your rendition of 'food, glorious food' was your best ever."

"What are you two gossiping about?" Eva said as she came in from the terrace carrying a pile of dishes.

"We were just saying how many people complimented the chef tonight."

"Really! Oh, that's lovely. The finger foods were a good idea and the crab ravioli was certainly a hit. It made me laugh to think that Mary had caught the crab last night and then served it to the customers today."

"You really can't get any fresher than that," Henrik said.

"Or more dedicated!" Eva laughed.

"I have some news to tell you," Samantha said as she joined them in the kitchen.

"Of course, we'll be with you in two seconds."

"Where's Lorenzo?" Mary asked, "Is he joining us?"

"He's gone back to bed. The exhaustion just

overwhelms him."

"Is he feeling better, Sam?" Martha asked.

"He is. The rest is helping enormously; you've all been so kind to him but it will take time. I can't believe how lucky he is to survive this awful virus. But he was in good shape before Covid struck so that has to be a good thing. Now I have some news for you and I am as surprised as you will be," She hesitated for a moment a feeling of embarrassement sweeping over her. "I'm pregnant with Lorenzo's baby."

She waited for a reaction, which was immediate. Martha instantly struggled to her feet.

"Come here, darling. This is the best news we could possibly have. I would never have guessed," Martha said. "When are you due?"

Sam laughed. "I have quite a big bulge, which is growing daily. The baby is due 18th September. She was suddenly inundated with hugs and good wishes, and tears of joy fell down her face. "Oh dear, I'm a bit emotional at the moment. These last few months have been so intense. When I had morning sickness, I thought I had Covid, and then I put it down to the emotional upset we were all experiencing. There just wasn't time to think about anything. I rarely saw Lorenzo. He was just so busy, hardly stopping to eat or sleep, and when he caught Covid and was hooked to the machines to keep him alive. I was so worried I didn't think he would make it."

With her arm around Sam, Mary stepped forward and led her to a chair.

'Now, you need to calm down. It's time to let us take care of you. Everything is going to be OK. Lorenzo will need time to recover, but we are all here for you, and whatever you decide, we will help you with your baby."

"Thank you everyone. I knew you would understand. At the moment, Lorenzo and I are just taking each day as it comes. We will bring the baby up together, but we need time to come to terms with everything that has happened."

"Of course you do, and it is wonderful news. Now you must make sure you don't over do things. You shouldn't be carrying heavy pots! Let us take care of you." John said.

"Really, I'm feeling fine. It's just great to be back in the restaurant. But I will give you a shout, John, if I need help."

At that moment Alfie sauntered into the kitchen, following the smell of food. He stopped and stared at everyone crowding around Samantha. Something was happening. He skilfully edged his way through the crowd and found Sam's legs, then he instinctively snuggled next to her, sensing that this was what she needed.

Brother Emmanuel's Fear

(Novita di Fratello Emmanuel)

Even with lockdown eased, Sorrento felt lonely and empty. A few shops slowly began to open, but the hotels remained closed. Foreign travel was difficult, and tourists faced similar problems in their own countries. The cobbled streets leading down to Marina Grande were silent. It felt like life had changed drastically, and someone had pressed the pause button.

Piazza Tasso was unaccustomed to peace and quiet. The restaurant tables and chairs, which had been stacked inside the buildings, were slowly being put out in the hope of attracting people to sit down and enjoy a coffee. Everyone wondered when they would once again be welcoming tourists back into their fine establishments for pizza and pasta. Not many people currently wanted coffee and Cannoli, Italy's favourite cake. The risk of catching COVID-19 was still real. Even the hot sun penetrating through the narrow, cobbled streets sending shadows dancing on the walls of the buildings added to the sadness and loneliness of a once thriving and passionate town.

It had been on Martha's mind to visit the monastery. She wanted to see how the monks were coping, particularly Brother Emmanuel, who she knew was getting frail. He greeted her at the monastery door with outstretched arms.

"Signora, please come in. It is a great pleasure to see you. Tell me, what brings you to the monastery? Is the Abbott expecting you?"

"No, he isn't. Now that lockdown has been lifted I wondered if I could visit Giovanni's grave? He has been on my mind. Would that be in order?"

"Of course, Signora. Please follow me. Our Garden of Rest is not far."

Martha followed him down the dark corridors. She noticed with sadness his difficulty in walking. The cold stone floors had taken their toll over the years on the old monk. She had always admired his positive attitude, but he seemed tired and weary today. She noticed that very little light was coming through the tiny windows. The sun, usually bright and cheerful, had become grey strips of cloudy, dusty air as it escaped through the cracks in the glass. Martha was relieved to step outside and breathe the fresh air. She shuddered slightly as a cool breeze came from nowhere, and she was grateful for her cotton jacket as she hugged it tightly to her body.

"Here we are." Brother Emmanuel said. "I tend the grave every day. Giovanni doesn't get any visitors."

"Not even his mother or sister?" Martha asked.

"No. I am the only one. But, Signora, I find it quite hard to come here. Sometimes I feel like he is watching me." The frail old monk lowered his voice. "The atmosphere is so strong. I have spoken to the Abbott about my feelings. I am finding it hard to forgive this boy for the pain he has caused."

"What has the Abbott advised?" Martha asked, surprised to hear the monk's sudden strong outburst.

"He says that I need to find peace with my thoughts and that prayer is the only answer. I have always believed this to be so, but from the first moment I met this young boy, I felt an evil emanating from him. And I cannot shake it off."

"You can't help your feelings, Emmanuel. However, you are wise to question your thoughts. It shows honesty to yourself, and I am sure eventually, you will find the peace you are looking for."

"Thank you, Signora. When you have chosen a life path of prayer and dedication, questioning your belief suddenly becomes a shock."

"Sometimes things happen in life just for that purpose. Humans are strange, complicated creatures, and I am not convinced everyone can be saved or forgiven." Martha whispered, "I think evil is amongst us and always has been. It is hard to forgive someone who has deliberately caused you harm."

The Brother clutched Martha's arm.

Yes, that is exactly how I feel."

A few moments later, Martha stared at a mound of earth and the simple wooden cross. As she placed a small spray of wildflowers on the grave she noticed Mary' silver necklace.

"Here is an example of forgiveness, Brother Emmanuel. Mary has found the strength to forgive Giovanni and has left him the necklace that seemed to trigger his hatred for her. Let's start by understanding this simple act of kindness."

I have tried, but I can feel the evil around me. It is like he is laughing at me and is waiting for me to react."

Martha felt a shiver go down her spine. She also felt an uneasy presence.

"Do you remember that night many years ago when you and your husband buried the German soldier?" The elderly monk suddenly blurted out.

Martha was visibly shaken by his remark.

"How did you know about it?" She whispered, a feeling of fear creeping into her voice.

"I saw you. I had been in the chapel, praying as I couldn't sleep, and as I walked back through the cloisters, I saw a figure in the cemetery, so I went to investigate. I heard you all talking about him and instantly knew who you were referring to."

"I didn't know you were at the monastery during the war,"

"Si Signora. I came here when I was 14 as a novice. It was 1943. My parents had been killed in the bombings in Napoli. The Church took me in, and the monks agreed to take me on, and I have been here ever since." The old monk wiped away a tear as he became emotional. "I shall be 91 in September. I am very old, Signora."

Martha placed her hand on his arm. "So am I, Signor," she said kindly.

Emmanuel continued, his memories flooding back.

"I remember vividly the German army being camped here in our beloved house of God. They were cruel to the brethren, laughing at them and often kicking them. I hid, scared for my life. One day, the Capitan found me hiding behind the altar. He dragged me out and... and," Emmanuel hesitated for a moment. He wiped his cheek as the tears came flooding down his face.

"Please don't cry. It was a long time ago. A lot of terrible things happened in those times." Martha said as she fought back the tears herself.

"No, I need to tell somebody." He whispered. "I've kept the shame of it to myself all these years." He slid to the floor, resting his arm on Giovanni's grave. "The Capitan, he ...he forced me.... he abused me..." the tears fell, and Martha knelt beside him, visibly shocked at his outburst.

"Hoffman, did a lot of bad things. It wasn't your fault. You have been violated against your will and in a place of God. How can I help you to forgive yourself?"

"I... I'm all right. Now I've spoken about it, I feel like the burden is lifting."

Martha spoke softly. "We also suffered under the Nazis. During the war, Capitan Hoffman controlled our daily lives. My father was forced to do things he didn't want any part of. Then, when it was over, life returned to normal until twenty years later, when he returned. My Papa had something the German wanted. He said he would return to claim it when Germany won the war. But we know they didn't, and it turned out that

Hoffman had been in prison for twenty years for war crimes." Martha hugged the old monk to her

'He tried to shoot my father, and Papa retaliated and went to defend himself, but the Nazi got shot. It was an accident. My father was horrified so my husband, George, took over, and we decided the best thing to do was to get rid of the body. We chose the monastery as a place where no one would find him. I had no idea you had seen us. I am so sorry for any grief we have caused you."

"I knew it was him. I heard you mention his name. I was pleased he was dead. He deserved his fate."

Martha muttered a simple prayer and took the Brother's arm to lead him away.

"Come, let us go inside. I am worried about you."

He turned and smiled. "Thank you, Signoria, for your kindness and understanding. I feel better having shared my feelings with you. But there is something else you should know. When the Abbot decided Giovanni should be buried here, he instructed the brothers to dig a grave a little away from the main graveyard. They chose the very place where you buried Capitan Hoffman. I was terrified that they would find some of his remains but, fortunately, they were interrupted by the beginnings of a thunderstorm, so they quickly dug a hole, and very soon Giovanni had been laid to rest over the Capitan. They didn't see anything suspicious." Brother Emmanuel waited for a response from the Signora. She couldn't entirely take in what he was saying.

"You mean they are both buried together in the same place?" It seemed incredulous to her that this coincidence should have occurred.

"Si, Signora. I think that is why tending the grave is so upsetting. The man I hated most in the world, who took my boyhood away from me, and a young man who also filled me with terror are together. I can feel their presence, yet I am drawn to the grave and find it hard to keep away. It is as though they are goading me."

My dear man. It is all those terrible memories haunting you. I can understand your fear. After all these years, you still cannot find peace in your heart to forgive those who were cruel to you. I wish I could help you. At this time in your life, you should be feeling calm and rested in your mind, not haunted by the past. Please visit me at The Villa anytime you are struggling to cope. We can enjoy afternoon tea together. Mary could join us and share her feelings about Giovanni and how she came to forgive him. As for Hoffman, what happened to you as a young boy is hard to forgive but you must stop blaming yourself."

"Grazie, you have helped me greatly today. Now the burden is lifted, I will pray peacefully tonight. And yes, it would be a great pleasure to visit again Signora. I will look forward to it."

"I am sure that John will call for you and ensure you are returned safely. Your old bicycle is ready for a rest."

Brother Emmanuel chuckled softly. "You are right, Signora. It has served me well, but I think our days of riding these hills are sadly ending."

Arm in arm, they strolled back to the entrance door. Both were lost in their own thoughts.

John was waiting for her outside the monastery doors. His business trip to Sorrento took less time than he thought. The air conditioning in the car was welcome after the heat of the day.

In the distance, he could hear the soothing chant of the monks as they walked towards their afternoon prayer. Staring up at the monastery walls, he was fascinated by the architecture. *'You must be a special person to dedicate your life to the Lord.'* He thought to himself. *'But it's the same as being in the army. You pledge yourself to safeguard your Queen and country.*

The trouble is it doesn't bring you the peace you thought it would. Pride and brotherhood with your mates, yes, but not peace of mind.' John laughed out loud. *'The answer to my problems would be to become a monk.'*

The ancient wooden doors creaked open, and Martha stepped out. She immediately put her hand over her eyes to shield herself from the brightness of the sunshine. John went to help her to the car.

"Thank you, John. I hope I haven't kept you waiting."

"Not at all. I've just been enjoying the quiet and contemplating joining the monastery. The monks must be truly at peace with themselves."

"Don't believe it, John. I'm afraid Brother Emmanuel is having very worrying thoughts."

"Really, what do you mean?"

"I shouldn't repeat his conversation, but you must keep it to yourself. He is frightened."

"What of?" John said as he manoeuvred the car down the rough track to the road below.

"Giovanni, to name one," Martha replied, waiting for a reaction, but none came. "He thinks his spirit is watching him."

John coughed. "I think I know how he feels. He's been following me ever since I first saw him." John thought for a moment as he allowed this news to sink in. "It makes you think, though. The world is in a bad state. Maybe all the sadness is penetrating through. I know I can feel it, and with Covid happening, I think everyone is on edge. I believe, Martha that some people give off an aura of evil. I've felt it in Afghanistan. It attaches itself and follows you around, and Giovanni was such a person." John set off down the country road towards home. "We need some good news and soon."

"We certainly do. As soon as more restrictions are lifted, I have invited Emmanuel to pop in for afternoon tea, and he may do so. Would you collect him? He is too old to be on his bicycle. I know the Abbott probably wouldn't approve of one of his monks indulging in the shameful sin of eating scones and cream. Still, the Abbott is not helping him to work out why he feels afraid, and just talking to him this afternoon, he was calming down a bit and definitely was interested in calling around."

"I will, Martha. He is a nice man, and he may be able

to help me anyway. I want to learn a little more about becoming a monk."

Martha laughed. "I think you would make a good addition to the monastery, John. They may be able to teach you how to grow grapes!"

Now that's a good idea, Martha. I need all the help I can get."

A Boat Trip to Capri
(Una Gita in Barca a Capri)

The extreme heat of the summer had been overwhelming, and most of the work on The Villa gardens and vineyard was carried out in the morning when the air was cool.

John was walking around the olive trees, assessing their progress. It was looking good. It filled his heart with pride when he saw the vegetation grow in front of him. Martha had said he had a magic touch, but he quickly mentioned he couldn't have done anything without the rich, fertile soil and the sunshine and rain.

He could hear someone calling his name. It was Franco.

"Ciao, Franco, what brings you here?"

"I'm waiting for Mary; she's chatting to Eva and Sam. Honestly, she said she would be five minutes. That was half an hour ago."

"That's women for you," John said.

"If you don't mind me saying so, John, you need the love of a good woman. Someone to bring you back to life. You are too serious, my friend."

"Well, it doesn't always work out as we want, Franco. I would love to meet someone so special that it makes each day worth living. But, to date, I am still looking."

"Don't worry, John, I think Mary has someone in mind for you. Make sure you come to my boat on Saturday night. We are having a party for everyone to celebrate the lifting of the lockdown restrictions. Mary wants to introduce you to a very nice woman."

John, surprised by this sudden invitation, was taken aback.

"Who has she in mind for me. Do I know her?"

"Her name is Chloe, and she is French. Mary and her have been friends for a long time since working together at British Airways. When the flights were stopped because of Covid, Chloe lost her job. She loves this area, so decided to live here and open a French cheese shop. Apparently, her family is into cheese in a big way, and she is a bit of an expert. I have met her, and I think you two have much in common."

"Really. My God, I don't know one word of French."

"Don't worry, she speaks English and Italian. I am sure you will get on well. After all, on my boat, you will have the moon, the stars, and a little bit of Italian romance to help you."

John looked quite horrified.

"Don't worry, John. Just turn up and let the magic happen on my love boat."

John laughed. "I can't turn that invitation down, Franco. I'll definitely be there."

***

Saturday evening arrived, and Franco proudly stood aboard his boat to welcome his guests.

Martha was wearing a beautiful vintage cotton dress, in deep yellow like the colour of sun kissed corn. She added a light pale lavender shawl around her to keep her warm from the sea breeze. Signor Miccio accompanied her. He had also dressed for the occasion in linen trousers, a white shirt with a navy sweater loosely tied around his neck. To complete his debonair look, he wore a Panama hat. The night promised a celebration of a little more freedom from the Government. Coronavirus was beginning to decline enough to warrant small gatherings of people.

Eva and Henrik arrived on their Vespa. They were laughing loudly.

"A party, at last," Eva shouted to everyone. She looked young and fresh in a long white shirt and ripped jeans. Henrik complimented her look by wearing exactly the same.

"Look at those two. How wonderful to be young again with a whole life to look forward to." Martha spoke quietly to Signor Miccio.

"Sono d'accordo, (I agree). They are a breath of fresh air. I love being in their company. Eva is a remarkable young woman, and Henrik, Oh, he reminds me of me when I was his age."

Eva stepped aboard the boat. "Hi everyone. Isn't this great? Papa, where are you taking us?"

"It's a lovely calm evening, perfect for sailing

around Capri. Does everyone agree?

"Of course," Mary shouted. "It's so hot; we need a swim."

"Calm down, Signora. Your husband has to get everyone aboard safely." Franco smiled.

John was last to arrive. "I'm sorry to be late. It's Alfie's fault. He ran away every time I tried to catch him."

"il est tellement delicieux (he is so delightful). Chloe said. "Look at his little scarf around his neck," she bent down to stroke him.

"John, let me introduce you to Chloe," Franco said as he smiled at both of them

"Bonjour, Chloe. It is a pleasure to meet you."

"Ciao, John. I love your little dog. He is so sweet."

"Not really, he can be very naughty. I'm hoping he will be on his best behaviour tonight."

"Oh, I think he will have a lovely evening." She laughed and looked at John, who was smiling broadly. He hadn't expected Chloe to be so pretty. Her chic style, impetuous smile, and dimpled cheeks instantly attracted him. He liked her. In return, Chloe was also weighing John up. Mary had told her he was serious and had a troubled life. Chloe's philosophy was to live life to the full. But her genuine, empathetic nature wanted to try and understand this man. So far, she liked him, especially the way he treated his dog, which confirmed he had a big heart.

Martha leaned back and relaxed in the sumptuous cushions.

"Signor Miccio, when did you first sail around Capri?"

"Ah, Signora, many, many moons ago. I think when I was a young man and in love with my very first girlfriend."

"Tell me more," She said. The glass of Prosecco was starting to have a relaxing effect on her. She was enjoying this moment and felt quite flirty and frivolous. Her dress made her feel like a young woman, not an old lady. After the confines of Covid, it was wonderful to feel free and attractive again.

"Her name was Caroline, and she was from a place called Kensington."

"I know it well. It is in London and very decadent."

"She was a beautiful woman. Perhaps a little bit older than myself, and she had an air of maturity but not old, just someone who had experienced life. I remember she had a beautiful smile similar to yours, Signora. In fact, you remind me of her. Elegant, I think, is the word I am looking for."

And this lady, was she married?"

"Her story is unfortunate. Her husband had died on a secret mission. She told me he was a spy. I'm unsure if I believed her, but it made her seem more interesting. I have to say she was a very passionate woman. She was also wealthy, so whatever her husband did for a living, he did it well."

"Goodness, Signor, what happened?"

"Oh, you know. I was a young man eager to learn the ways of the world, and Caroline was an excellent teacher. We had a lot of fun together, but she had to return to London when her husband was killed. We promised to keep in touch, but it wasn't to be, and then I met Vivienne."

"Oh, my goodness. Do you know, I am not sure if you are making this up," She laughed.

An innocent look crossed his face. "Signora, I am an Italian man, full of passion and love. I would not know how to make up such stories."

Mary interrupted their conversation.

"Franco suggests we stop at the little bay just before Capri town in case anyone wants to swim. Is that OK with you both?"

"Of course it is, but I will stay here," Martha replied. "Would you like a swim, Signor?"

"I would indeed. I have been looking forward to it."

"Good, we will be there in a few minutes. Martha, would it be all right if you look after Alfie? John doesn't want him to go in the water. It is very deep here."

"Of course I will."

"I'll put his lead on and bring him over. Thanks."

"No problem." She turned to Signor Miccio. "Take care. Although the water seems very calm tonight, it can be quite treacherous in places."

"Don't worry, Signora. I am a very strong swimmer. I will be careful, I promise."

Martha settled back to watch as they dived and jumped in the cool water. She hadn't swum for years, ever since her younger sister, Agnetta, had drowned when she was a teenager. It had happened during a family outing at Capo di Sorrento. A powerboat had come speeding around the rocks, and her poor sister, who was sunbathing, was washed into the water. Martha's brothers and father jumped in to save her, but it was too late. The effect on her family was devastating. The post-mortem revealed that Agnetta had probably hit her head on the sharp rocks, a tragic accident.

For Valentina, losing her daughter had broken her heart, and the light seemed to disappear from her. Martha tried hard to help her mother recover, but the grief was too intense. The whole family struggled to comprehend how it could have happened on such a lovely summer's day. The dark clouds of sadness had descended on the family and hung around for many years.

Being close to water always brought the anxiety back to Martha, and she was relieved when they all came safely back on board. She was glad they had enjoyed their swim, and she could start to relax again and join in with the laughing and singing. It was a memorable moment, surrounded by the deep blue water and the sheer beauty of Capri with its colourful buildings, which enticed visitors to its shore.

Mary sat next to her. "It's been a long time since we have been able to have so much fun. Thank goodness Covid is calming down a bit. We can start making plans again and look forward to the future. What do you think, Martha?"

"Yes, darling. Hopefully, life can return to normal, and we can welcome our guests from abroad again."

Signor Miccio sat down next to the two women. He was wrapped in a big towel and was grinning from ear to ear.

"How did you enjoy your swim?" Martha asked.

"It was wonderful, Signora. To feel the cool water on such a hot day is perfection. It has been far too long since I went swimming on Capri."

"I think you work too hard. When the hotel reopens, you should spend more time doing things you enjoy. You can always swim in the cove at The Villa."

"I will be so happy when the hotel reopens. It is my life. I live for nothing else than to welcome back my friends and new visitors to your wonderful hotel, Signora."

"I know," Martha replied. "I think we have all missed the tourists."

Eva shouted out. "Food is ready if you want to help yourself."

They didn't need telling twice as they piled their plates high with barbecued fish and gazed out over the stunning scenery, each one quietly enjoying the serenity of the moment.

A New Life
(Una Nuova Vita)

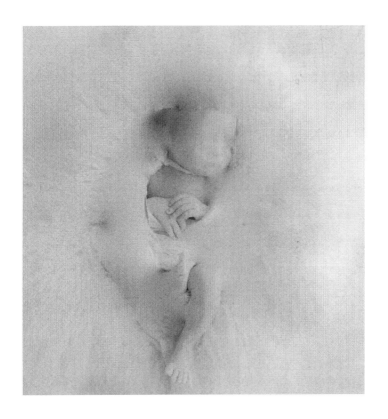

Quietness had descended on The Villa. The rush of excitement as everyone gathered in the courtyard before setting off to Capri had evaporated. Samantha waved goodbye and stood quietly, wondering how to spend the rest of her day. She had declined to go with them as she was getting close to her due date, and the thought of the motion of the boat didn't appeal to her.

Lorenzo had gone to Napoli for a meeting with the medical board. His recovery from Covid was slow, but there was a significant improvement, and his spirits were definitely lifting. He was hoping to return to work. There was still a lot to be done. Covid hadn't gone away.

Sam decided on a slow walk down to the cove. August had been very hot and this continued into September. The sea breeze was cool and inviting. It had been a long time since she could go down to her quiet place. The opportunity to have a moment alone, to think and take in all that had happened, was not to be missed. Life had been a roller coaster of change, and with Covid, it had added panic in everyone's mind that was hard to shake off. The fear and worry was still there despite the hope of a vaccine being distributed in a few months. It was a case of being vigilant and safe.

She grabbed a couple of towels from the linen cupboard and filled her beach bag with a bottle of water and some cake. It occurred to her that she couldn't stop eating cake because her baby was demanding sweet things. Well, that was her excuse, and she was sticking to it. With her phone in her pocket, she was ready to go.

The walk down the lane was relatively sheltered from the blistering heat. The large green foliage was interspersed with wildflowers. She picked a few to scatter on the water in Robbie's memory. Through the hedges, she could see glimpses of the deep turquoise of the Mediterranean. The perfume of flowers wafted gently in the breeze, and the display of pink, blue, and yellow wildflowers exploded into the atmosphere.

Samantha stood in a clearing and was mesmerised when she spotted Franco's lugger boat. Its terracotta sails drifting towards Capri and complimenting the azure blue water. She waved in the hope they would see her.

Her memory began taking her to a moment last year when she had walked this same path after deciding to scatter Robbie's ashes in the cove. If she had known that Giovanni, the young stalker, had been watching her every move, she may have reconsidered. It was a very special moment in her mind, and today, she was looking forward to spending some spiritual time with her late husband. There was a lot of confusion in her head, and she hoped to get some clarity to move on with her life.

Since Robbie's death, she had struggled to let go of him. The feeling that he was watching over her was comforting. Being a nurse, she encountered death many times, but it wasn't until she had experienced loss herself that she understood how powerful the emotion was.

Holding loved ones close was preferable to letting go of them forever. Sam had stared into the faces of the dying. Watching the light go from them and realising that only their physical body remained empty, shrivelled and cold. At some stage before the finality of death, she knew their soul had moved on from this world to somewhere she didn't understand. But she needed Robbie's physical presence to touch and hold her. His spiritual voice had guided her, letting her know when he was ready to be free. She had carefully released his ashes into the cove's calm, tranquil water and silently swam with them as she said her goodbyes. It had been a memorable moment that would stay with her all her life. She felt he still looked after her, bringing her comfort and strength.

As she gazed at the calm, gentle waves, she was compelled to be with him one last time. Carefully removing her dress and caressing her stomach, she slowly waded into the warm sea. It felt wonderful to be in tune with her body and nature. Robbie's voice came into her head, kind and loving.

'Darling Sam, you must not worry about me anymore. The time is here now for you to love again and follow a path of your choice for the future. I have been watching you. I am so proud of how you put everyone before yourself, even to risk your own safety, and now look at you about to bring into this crazy world a new human being."

"But what about Lorenzo?" Sam said. "I didn't mean to let you down. I was missing you so much?"

"Sam, listen to yourself. Lorenzo is a good person. The love we had together belongs only to you and me. I'm so sorry it didn't last long, but I think it was more special. Lorenzo loves you greatly, but he knows it is your life, and only you can decide your future. Now is the time to stop putting others first and to think about yourself."

The tears began to fall down her face, mixing with the seawater.

'Don't cry, Sam. I understand and want you to know that even if you and Lorenzo get together, I will always be here for you if you want me to. You

only have to ask. I'm your guardian angel and also that of your baby. Everything is good."

The sun broke through the thin cloud and showered her with a shimmering glitter of golden light. She radiated in this extraordinary moment as she realised what she wanted to do with her future. Carefully making her way to the small beach, she dressed and lay back on her towel, her long blonde hair drying in the sunshine and the warmth enfolding her body. Soon, she was sleeping calmly without dreams or worry.

An hour slipped by, and a sudden sharp pain brought Samantha out of her sleep.

For a moment, she lay hardly daring to move. The pain was deep in her back, and it didn't feel like the baby was kicking. Instead, it felt like it was ready to come into the world.

She quickly reached for her phone and rang Lorenzo. There was no answer.

***

Lorenzo was battling through the heavy traffic in the heart of Naples. The afternoon's heat was intense, and tiredness was starting to sweep over him. He was pleased; the meeting had gone well, and the hospital's directors had been very welcoming. They showered him with praise for his work in Bergamo and everything he had accomplished in helping to save lives. Being a modest man, Lorenzo didn't want praise. He just wanted to feel better and to get back to work immediately.

Queues were forming at the entrance to the autostrada. He sighed. One thing he hadn't been looking forward to was the drive to Naples every day for work. He had thought about relocating nearer the hospital, but The Villa had seduced him with its charm and calmness, and he had realised that he needed it desperately.

He sat in the endless queue, his thoughts turning to Samantha. From the first moment he met her, he knew she was the one. He loved her with every beat of his heart but knew she was still vulnerable after Robbie's death, and he realised that patience and time would be his best hope for her to love him back.

The traffic started to move quickly, and soon, he was passing the suburbs of Castellamare di Stabia and heading for the tourist region of Sorrento. The scenery changed from industrial working towns to an emerging oasis of stunning beauty. The pine spruce trees, with their distinctive umbrella shape, structured the Italian landscape, and each bend revealed a panoramic vista of glistening sea dotted with colourful yachts.

He used to love this drive, but now he felt lonely. She wasn't sitting next to him, and for the first time in his life, he knew he didn't want to be alone anymore.

His phone began to light up, and realising it was Sam, he answered quickly.

"Ciao, Sam, come va? (How is it going?)

"Help, I need help. I'm in labour, and I'm alone down at the cove. I can't make it back up the hill."

"Dio mio." (Oh my God!) He hesitated for a moment, a feeling of helplessness coming over him. "Where exactly are you?"

"I've managed to get to the water's edge, and my lower body is lying in the shallow end. It's easing the pain a bit."

"Look, Sam, I'll ring for an ambulance. I'm just driving through Vico Equense, so it will take at least 30 minutes to get to you. The traffic is crazy. I'll ring you back to let you know when someone can be with you."

He immediately dialled the ambulance service only to be told there was a delay due to a serious accident on the road to Positano. Thinking quickly, he rang John's number and breathed a sigh of relief when he answered.

"John, it's Lorenzo. Samantha needs help. She has gone into labour but is down by the cove and can't get back up the hill. I'm at least half an hour away. Where are you? Can you help her?"

"We are on the boat on our way back from Capri. Gosh, I can't believe this. She was fine when we left her this morning. What about an ambulance?"

"No, there is none available. Are you there, John? I can't hear you."

"Yes, I was just telling Franco. We are heading to the cove now; we are about fifty minutes away. We can moor the boat in the deep water, and Mary and I will use the dinghy to get to her."

"That's good, thanks. I'll ring her back to say help is on the way."

"Great, Don't worry. She will be OK."

'Si, si, grazie." As he phoned Sam back, he was aware of the beating in his heart. He was going to be a father. He must get there to help his child come into the world. "Sam, are you there? The phone line crackled and then went dead.

***

When Lorenzo phoned with news of Sam, everyone was watching as the sun began to fade in the sky, a soft pink light appearing on the surface of the sea. Capri looked bathed in a rose-coloured glow. Only the sound of John's phone ringing broke the magic spell. They could hear the urgency in his voice, and it was pretty obvious that something was happening.

"That was Lorenzo," John said. "Samantha is in difficulties down at the cove. The baby is coming. We are turning the boat around and heading back to help."

"Oh my goodness," Martha said. "The poor girl, she is all alone."

"How long, Franco, will it take to get to her?" Mary asked.

"Forty-five minutes, I think, and Lorenzo is nearer, so he should get there before us."

"That's good. I'm sure everything will be fine." Mary said as she tried to smile reassuringly to everyone, but she was secretly wishing they were nearly there.

***

Twenty-five minutes later, Lorenzo stopped in a cloud of dust outside The Villa's forecourt. Grabbing his medical bag, he headed down the track to the cove. His sudden burst of energy took his breath away, and he slowed to a pace he could manage without collapsing.

He gasped when he saw her. She was lying half in the water, a large pool of blood surrounding her, but she was conscious and hugging her newborn baby close to her breast. Sam looked up as she heard him shout her name. He knelt down next to her and quickly assessed the situation.

"You are OK, Sam. You've lost some blood, but it's stopped. I've just clamped the cord. How is baby doing?"

"Look for yourself." She smiled. "Lorenzo, say hello to your daughter." Pulling back the towel she had wrapped her baby in to keep her dry she held her out to her father.

There was no way Lorenzo could hold back his tears. He had tried hard to control his emotions since Covid and his illness, but now they erupted, and the tears flowed. Wonderment flooded his face as he stared into his baby girl's eyes. He leaned over and gently kissed her and then turned to Samantha. "Grazie mia cara, grazie. She is perfect."

Only the sound coming from the dinghy as it

came into the cove and the shouts from John broke the spell between them.

"Let's get you both home and to bed," Lorenzo whispered gently.

"Over here, John," he shouted as the small craft entered the cove.

Mary was the first out, and she half swam and half waded towards them.

"Let me look," she cried. "Oh my, what a beautiful little face. It's a girl. I knew it would be a girl. Look at her hair! My word, she is gorgeous. And how are you feeling, Sam? You look amazing."

Samantha smiled. The relief and worry of giving birth alone had passed. It couldn't have gone better. To have her baby in the cove where she had shared her love and emotion with Robbie and then for Lorenzo to be part of her life was wonderful.

"Come on, darling, we must get you warm and dry," Mary said, her practical head taking over the situation. "Lorenzo, hold your daughter, and John, can you carry Sam to the boat?"

"Of course, just yell out if you are in pain or anything," John said as he lifted her gently.

"I've only had a baby, John. I'll be fine." Sam replied.

"I don't know anything about mothers and babies, so I'm not taking any chances. You cling on to me, and I promise I won't drop you."

Samantha was soon in the dinghy and heading for Franco's boat. Many coloured lights flashed in the sky as a local fiesta celebrated with fireworks. Samantha looked back at the little cove, and for a brief moment, she thought she saw Robbie waving to her. In her mind, she waved back, refusing to be sad. He would always be with her, but the time had come to move forward with her life and her new family.

Settling In
(Sistemarsi)

The newcomer to The Villa changed everything. Suddenly, the house was alive with the chatter and noise a new baby brings. Samantha recovered quickly; at first, this tiny bundle made her anxious. Her main concern was to keep her baby safe. Lorenzo took to being a father straight away. Everything came naturally to him as he cuddled and cossetted his daughter. His soft singing voice lulled her to sleep, whereas with Samantha she became stressed and immediately rushed to attend to her crying baby.

"Non preoccuparti, Sam," (don't worry). It's pretty normal to feel as you do. Babies demand so much from the mother."

"But, she is different with you. Somehow, you have the knack of getting her to sleep."

Martha, overhearing the conversation, said.

"It's because the baby feels safe in strong arms. All they need is to feel secure and warm and, of course, well-fed. You are doing brilliantly,

Samantha dear. I don't know anything about babies, but when my younger sister, Agnetta, was born, my mother struggled to settle her. It was all right after a few weeks."

"I know. I just don't want to do anything wrong."

"Darling, you need to rest more. Why don't you go and lie down? You've been through so much this year. Lorenzo and I will look after Rosa.

Samantha was grateful for the opportunity. She felt exhausted and took herself off to bed for several hours.

"How about a walk, Lorenzo?"

"Si, Signora. I'll get the carrozzina (pram)."

Together, they set off on a gentle stroll.

"I didn't know you had a sister. Is she still alive?" Lorenzo asked.

"No, sadly, she died when she was only 13. We had been to Capo di Sorrento, and Agnetta was lying on the rocks when a speedboat came around the bend. The sudden rush of water washed her off the rocks, and we couldn't save her."

"Martha, that is so sad. I can't imagine what it

is like to have siblings, but to lose one of them must be devastating."

"It was. Agnetta was so spirited and very beautiful. She loved life and brought fun into my parent's world, especially after the war. They were both heartbroken, and they blamed themselves, which was wrong. It was just a freak accident. It could have happened to anybody."

"It does make you think if life and death are just random. Maybe we are born with a date engraved in our souls, and when the time comes, nobody can save us. It's destiny."

"Goodness, I hadn't thought about it like that. Some people caught Covid and died, others survived, and some didn't even get it at all. It doesn't make sense."

Lorenzo sighed deeply. "We are so lucky to have come through it alive and can enjoy this beautiful place." He looked around at the abundant display of colour, from the lemons on the trees to the deep purple of the bougainvillea as it cascaded down the wooden trellis. "I find it amazing that nature continues to blossom amid a disease that could wipe out most of us. It's like this nightmare is not happening."

"I know what you mean," Martha said. "During lockdown, I would walk around the gardens, and all I could hear were birds singing. Gone was the noise of traffic and planes. Everywhere was silent. The population was locked away, not daring to touch anybody. I loved it. There was a peace that I hadn't encountered before, but the world continued to revolve. I'm sure if humans were wiped out, everything else would continue as normal."

"It certainly has been an alarming experience for all of us. It may be a wake-up call to remind us that life is fickle and we should enjoy our time here."

"Shall we sit down for a moment, Lorenzo? The baby is fast asleep?"

"Yes, under the shade of this olive tree would be nice. Isn't it beautiful? It must be 200 years old." He wiped the wooden bench clear of debris from the tree.

"I think it is. Look at the twisted trunk. It's like a

sculpture." Martha looked at Rosa and smiled. "I am so delighted you chose her name. Samantha told me you liked the idea of Rosaria or Rosa because she looks like an English Rose. Did you know it was my grandmother's name?"

"No, I had no idea. Well, that is very fitting."

"Yes, it is. My nonna was a wonderful woman. I remember her with much love. My goodness, she would have eaten Rosa alive with kindness. I didn't have any children. But I have been lucky in other ways. I have always found love." Martha said as she smiled at Rosa. "She has so much to look forward to, caring parents and a world that still looks after and appreciates old people and olive trees; she is a lucky girl. May I ask? Do you worry about her future?"

"Yes, Martha, I do. It was a shock to me when Samantha told me she was pregnant. I felt guilty, not only for persuading her to come to Bergamo and risking her life but to discover she was having my child, but also the world is very challenging and dangerous. Of course, that feeling was very brief. The thought of me being a father was something I had longed for, and my heart wanted to explode with pride."

"Ah, babies tend to arrive when least expected. I remember when I was a child. The world was devastated, ripped to shreds by the bombings and killing of war, but babies still continued to be born and survived throughout the horror."

"I cannot imagine how you all lived through that nightmare. From what I have read about the war, it is amazing how the world recovered, and you all found the strength to carry on."

"It is all you can do when you don't have a choice. Today, a killer virus is sweeping the world, but we continue. We laugh and cry. Sadly, not much hugging is going off, which I find particularly difficult. At least during the war, we could hold each other."

Lorenzo immediately put his arm around Martha.

"Ah, that's better. I was hoping you would do that."

"Martha, you are naughty." He laughed. "Seriously though, I think the vaccine will be the turning point. If it doesn't work, we are in serious trouble. Already the virus is beginning to show signs of spreading again."

"Yes, I did hear that on the radio. Do you think we will have to go through it all again?"

"Locking down the country is the only way to stop the virus from spreading. When I went to Naples the other day, my boss at the hospital asked me if I would consider being in charge of the Sorrento Hospital to prepare for the second wave and organize the vaccine rollout in this area when it is approved. Everyone in the country will be eligible to be vaccinated. It is a major task."

"Goodness, Lorenzo. I had no idea. I've drifted into a little world of my own. I forget that people are trying to save us from something we don't understand. Do you feel well enough to accept this job? It's going to be very tiring?"

"I have already accepted it after carefully thinking about it. My health is improving, and the fact that I would be based here in Sorrento is wonderful, especially being close to Samantha and Rosa. I think it's a great opportunity for me."

"I think so too. Travelling to Naples daily would be tiring, and I think Samantha needs you close by."

"We have discussed it, and she agrees that it would be good for me to be involved in the next stage of this awful pandemic. I have learnt much about the illness and can help the people here regarding the vaccine; it will be a challenge. Still, I've already started making arrangements for possible venues to be set up to administer it, and we also need trained staff. So that is a big commitment. At the moment, though, we are waiting for Britain and other countries to complete their testing, and then it will be all systems go."

The baby woke and stared out with wide eyes.

"Here we go. Our little princess is demanding attention." Martha laughed.

Alfie, who had come along on the walk, started to growl as the baby opened her mouth to let out a shrill cry. A sudden bark from him, and Rosa became silent.

"Look at that," Lorenzo cried. "Alfie knows how to keep her quiet. I must tell Samantha she does not need to worry anymore. Just put Alfie in charge."

Martha laughed. "It's lovely having a baby in the house. It makes everything seem so normal. Shall we head home for some refreshments?"

"Perfect, Martha. Let's go and eat Eva's cake she was baking this morning."

Grape Harvest
(Vendemmia)

John had befriended Angelo, an experienced wine producer, who was employed on a temporary basis to help him with the vineyard. He was intrigued to see how expertly Angelo cared for the tangled shoots. His knowledge was exactly what John needed, and before long, they had formed a good friendship. Over the summer months, as restrictions allowed, Angelo worked hard on the vines, and now the day had come when the grapes were ready to be picked.

The long rows of vines heavy with the weight of swollen, ripe, juicy fruit revealed the success of the past year's hard work of erecting poles, planting, fertilizing, irrigating, and spraying. John had never felt such excitement and couldn't wait to get on with the grape harvest. The baskets were lined up, and all volunteers were eagerly waiting to begin the winemaking process. It was backbreaking work, especially as the weather was sweltering. Everyone agreed it was thrilling to cut a beautiful bunch of red and green grapes with the thinning shears and drop them in the baskets, ready to be taken to Angelo's winery for crushing. A grape crusher machine was then used to separate the fruit and stem; the stems were cleaned, and the grape was crushed and sent to the pulp for further processing.

"Angelo, vienni qui (come here)," John shouted. "Do you think we will get it done in time? The weather is set to change later this week."

"Non preoccuparti, John," (Don't worry). You have done everything possible to help nature create an excellent crop. You can drink a glass of your own wine very soon. Even if we have to work through the night, we will do so."

John slapped his friend on the shoulder. "Thank you, Angelo. That means a lot to me."

"Ah, John, I am not saying you will enjoy your glass of wine. That may be in a year or two, but honestly, you are on the way to being a wine producer and owner of a vineyard."

John laughed. "Yes," he cried as he punched the air. "This is what I need to hear."

"Well, we have many hours of work ahead of us before we can celebrate. Andiamo." (Let's go)

Back in The Villa, preparations were made to serve the workers with big platters of spaghetti washed down with a local wine. Eva was in her element.

"Ti Amo Sorrento." She yelled out loud. "I love Sorrento, and I love my kitchen."

Henrik laughed at her. "I agree. This is the life. Cooking pasta in a traditional Italian kitchen. I never would have dreamt I would be doing this."

He hugged her, and together, they danced around the room, waving spoons and singing loudly.

Samantha was standing in the doorway watching them.

"You two are meant for each other." She laughed. "I don't want to spoil your fun, but your sauce is boiling over."

"Mamma Mia," Henrik yelled. "la salsa, la salsa!" (the sauce, the sauce). He kissed Eva and rushed to the stove, waving his wooden spoon.

"Do you need any help?" Sam asked as she

piled more juicy peaches into a bowl.

"I think everything's ready, Sam. I can hear them coming up from the vineyard. We just need to serve it."

"Come on then, I can't wait to return to normal and work in the restaurant again. Pass me the spaghetti, Signorina."

The long wooden table was laid out with fresh bread and salad. Samantha placed a steaming bowl of pasta in the centre of the table. It was only a short time before everyone was enjoying lunch. After a short rest, Angelo insisted it was time to return to work. There was so much to do. It was a race against the clock before the weather came in. He glanced at John. He was such an interesting guy. What had brought him to Italy and this way of life, he wondered? He was a mystery. But one thing was sure: he had a passion for wine, and Angelo desperately wanted to help him achieve his dream.

After a couple of days, the grapes were picked and sent to the processing unit. It wasn't long before John held a glass of the rich red grape juice in his hand. Tentatively, he took a sip.

"Oh my God, it's awful!" he cried.

"Angelo laughed. "Of course it is, John. Now we have added yeast to the juice, and it will start the fermentation process, which will take around two to three weeks to complete. Otherwise, it will be too acidic and not good."

"I was aware, but I hoped, by some miracle, it would be perfect. Never mind. We've done it. We have the harvest in, and soon, it will be in bottles stacked on the shelves of the wine cellar. It is a very proud moment for me, Angelo. Grazie millie, for all your help."

"Piacere mio, John," (my pleasure).

"So, what next?"

"Lots of clearing up to prepare the vines for the winter; in a few weeks, it will be time for the olive harvest and making the oil."

"Goodness, I have much to learn about being a rural farmer."

"It is the best feeling in the world when the crops are in. Then it is time to celebrate."

John threw his wine to the floor. *"One step at a*

time," he thought. *"This time next year, it will be drinkable."*

Mary's Heart Break
(Il Cuore Spezzato di Maria)

Although Mary and Franco had been working hard fishing at night and delivering fresh fish to the residents of Sorrento, they also had a lot of fun. Being together, alone on the water in the middle of the night, had been so precious to both of them, and tonight was no different. For the first time in twenty years they now had the chance to really spend time together

They had spread their nets quite close to Capri. Franco knew the waters and their dangerous currents and was careful not to put Mary in danger.

On the horizon they could see the constant flashing of lightning. The ending of a hot summer often bought a spectacular fireworks display created by nature. Dark clouds quickly began to form above the horizon, and Franco did not like the look of them.

"I think, Maria, we should give up tonight. We don't want to be out here. A storm is coming quite quickly. The waters are already choppy. I'll get the nets in, and we'll call it a day."

"OK, skipper," Mary, laughed. "You're the boss."

They returned to shore and were soon warm and cosy in their little apartment in Marina Grande overlooking the tiny habour. Darkness filled the room as a power cut affected the whole town. Lightning streaked across the skies, and the rumble of thunder echoed down the cobbled streets. Mary lit candles, and they opened a bottle of red wine and sat by the open window to watch the storm. She wrapped her arms around Franco's neck and leaned in to kiss him lightly on the neck.

"We got back just in time."

"We did, woman, come let us go to bed and enjoy the night." Franco laughed as he led her to the bedroom. The storm and wine had created a perfect evening for love. They lay in each other's arms, as the night wore on their passion became like the distant rumble of thunder. The occasional flash of lightning sent Mary closer to Franco for protection.

He laughed. "I don't believe it, Maria, you are afraid of the thunderstorm."

"I'm not at all. I just wanted to be closer to you."

"Ah, I don't believe you. There is no need to be afraid. I am here, and I will always protect you."

For once, Mary relaxed and allowed him to become the dominant partner. Not for long, just for this evening.

"Isn't Samantha's baby beautiful?" Franco said a short while later.

"Yes, she is a darling. I can't take my eyes off her." A tear began to trickle down Mary's face, and suddenly, she gave way to deep sobs.

"Cara, what is it. What is the matter?"

"Nothing, it's the wine. I drank it too quickly."

"No, it is more than that. Dimmi (tell me)"

"It could have been our baby." She burst out. The tears now pouring down like the rain outside the window.

"Non capisco (I don't understand)"

"When I left you years ago to return to London, I was pregnant."

"What! Madre di Dio (mother of god). Why didn't you tell me?"

"I didn't know until a few weeks later. You remember that night in Montepertuso, when we were having dinner. I asked if you had told your mother and family about me, and you hesitated. I knew then I was just your English girlfriend, and I wasn't prepared to be your secret lover. You know that was the reason why I left. Only a few weeks later, when I returned to England, I realised I was having your baby. But I didn't. I miscarried at 20 weeks, and I lost our child."

"Oh, Maria, Maria. I had no idea. My poor darling, I am so sorry. If I had known, I would have come for you."

"But that is the point, Franco. You knew my childhood was loveless. All I really crave for is to be loved for me, not for pity, but for who I am."

"I realise that now. I was a young, foolish boy who was infatuated with love. No, I mean sex. That was until I met you and knew I was in love with you. I just wasn't grown up enough to put you before my mother. I was stupid, and I paid a heavy price. Just like you did. I can't tell you how sorry I am, and I would do anything to put it right. Anything."

She sighed deeply and moved closer into his arms. The thunder dwindled away into the distance, the storm passed, and Mary, now calm again, kissed the man who had captured her heart all those years ago. Holding each other tight they drifted back to sleep. Their sad memories dwindled. They had found each other again and that was all that mattered.

Coronavirus Returns

(Il Coronavirus Ritorna)

Every day, new Covid cases were on the increase. The population had adhered to all the restrictions imposed on it. Distancing, facemasks, and stringent hygiene methods had been re-introduced to help control the numbers. Like most countries in Europe, the resurgence of COVID-19 had been expected.

Lorenzo was outside on the terrace. He could hear the agitated conversation coming from the kitchen. Signor Miccio's voice was the loudest.

"Mamma Mia, not another lockdown. What is to become of us?" he cried.

Niente panico" (don't panic). We know what we have to do. We coped the first time, and now we must take a deep breath and accept it is the only way to get back to normal." John calmly voiced his opinion.

"John is right, Eva said. "We will go back to the takeaway meals and baking bread."

"And we mustn't forget the vaccine is getting

very close to being administered. There is hope." Lorenzo said as he entered the kitchen and joined in the conversation. "I know it's frightening, but we must remain calm and vigilant. We have to protect each other, and sadly, with that in mind, I've decided to move out of The Villa and rent a place near the hospital in Sorrento. I'm returning to work in a couple of days, and I will be dealing directly with Covid patients and very soon the vaccine. I just can't risk passing it on to any of you. I've discussed it with Sam, and she agrees it's the right thing to do."

"Then you must do it. We'll all be here to help with the baby, and hopefully, it won't be too long, and then you can come home again. There is just one thing that bothers me," Martha said. "You haven't fully recovered from Covid yourself. What are the risks of you catching it again?"

"We don't know, Martha. But there are many doctors and nurses who are in the same position as me. Also, we do have improved PPE. I promise I'm not afraid and will be very careful."

A short while later, Samantha was helping

Lorenzo pack.

"I wish I could do something. I feel a bit of a fraud."

"Don't be silly, Sam. You have Rosa to care for. That is a more important job."

She laughed and went to give him a big hug. They clung together, their lips brushing, and then their kiss deepened.

"I love you," she whispered. "Please take care and come back to me."

These were the words he had been waiting for. "I've waited so long to hear you say that. Anche io ti amo." (I love you too).

She smiled as they clung together tightly.

"Let me come with you to get you settled in. Rosa and I want to see your apartment to make it comfortable for you."

"Yes, please do. It's pretty close. I can drive you back."

After loading his suitcases into the car, including a considerable amount of food Eva had packed for him in boxes, they set off down the winding road towards Sorrento.

"Where is the apartment, Lorenzo?" Sam asked as they passed the Grand Hotel Excelsior Vittoria and were in the main square.

'It's just here. Above the ice cream parlour."

They opened the wooden door leading into a large courtyard. A modern bicycle was propped up against an ancient Roman statue. Sam smiled at the mishmash of the old world blending with the new. A stone staircase led to the apartment door. Inside was a traditional kitchen and sitting room. A bedroom and a shower room were on the next floor. It was adequately furnished with very dark pieces of furniture and above the iron bed was a traditional Italian painting of Jesus on the cross. Everywhere was spotlessly clean.

Samantha put the baby down in the centre of the bed. Rosa was sleeping peacefully, having just been fed.

"Oh, look at this," Sam cried as she opened the French shutters and stepped out onto a small wrought- iron balcony.

"It's perfect, Lorenzo, Come and look. It overlooks Piazza Tasso. You'll be able to see

Mary and Franco delivering their fish and Henrik and Eva when they set up the bread stall again. It's wonderful. They'll be able to wave to you, and then I know you will be safe. Where does this lead?" she asked as she approached a small iron spiral staircase.

"I'm not sure. It's the first time I've seen the apartment. You go and look. I'll stay here with Rosa."

She skipped up the staircase, already feeling excited. The wooden door led to a small roof terrace, and in front of her was a beautiful sea view. A few pieces of furniture were tucked away under a sloping roof.

"Lorenzo, it's brilliant. It's a roof terrace overlooking the sea. It is perfect for you to have your coffee in the mornings. You will love it."

He popped his head around the door and was delighted to have a small outdoor space where he could breathe the fresh air.

I think I will be reasonably happy here," he said. "It has everything I need. Can you see The Villa?"

"I can see the top rooms and roof. I love it. I could live here. It's great overlooking the piazza. Unfortunately, there won't be anything going off outside. No tourists because of lockdown, but at least it will be quiet, and you will get some sleep."

"Apart from the church bells, Sam."

She laughed. "Being Italian, you should be used to them. Now, let's look to see if you need anything else."

"Only you!" he said as he joined her on the terrace. "Ho bisogno solo di te" (I need only you.) he repeated.

***

With the continued resurgence of COVID-19 throughout Italy, European governments introduced a traffic light system to notify citizens of the areas seriously affected. Hospitals in Naples were experiencing unprecedented numbers of patients admitted to intensive care and hospitalisation. Lorenzo was again in the danger zone. His health had improved, but he was still prone to flare-ups of exhaustion. His superiors were grateful for his expertise, but they insisted he worked only a normal working day and went home to sleep. Despite his protests, he knew they were right. He had agreed to work in Naples during this new emergency, and he was pleased when, at the beginning of December, he was transferred back to the Sorrento Hospital to be in charge of the immunisation programme.

His temporary home above the ice cream parlour was a sanctuary for him, and each evening, he sat on the roof terrace, wrapped up against the cool nights, watching the sunset over the sea. His thoughts turned to Samantha. His body ached for her, and the physical isolation was hard to bear. How much longer can this agony go on for, he wondered? He was desperate for normality and a life with her and his baby. He glanced towards The Villa in the distance and wondered if she too was thinking about him.

As it happened Lorenzo was very much in her thoughts. Mary and Martha were bathing Rosa so Sam stepped outside on the balcony. She smiled at the laughter that came from the bathroom.

"*Someone's having fun,*" *she thought "and I don't think its just Rosa.*" It would so nice if Lorenzo was here too. He would love this interaction. Rosa was now nearly three months old and with her big blue eyes and blond hair she was becoming a beautiful baby.

One morning, he sat on his balcony in the kitchen enjoying a bowl of fresh fruit. His eyes wandered over to Piazza Tasso. The Fauno Bar opposite his building was open for a short while. He could see one or two people inside, but gone were the hoards of tourists who would sit outside on a balmy summer's evening, laughing and enjoying the music and food. Tourists looked forward to being part of the atmosphere of the piazza, which looked liked an impressionist painting. A voice called up to him.

"Lorenzo, can you hear me?" He glanced down to see John waving madly. "Ciao, John. Is everything OK?"

"Yes, don't worry, everyone is well. Samantha

sends her love, and she wanted you to know that Rosa is very settled and happy, although they are both missing you."

"Grazie, John, for the news. Tell her I love her, no wait, tell her I miss her so much, and no, tell her I am well and missing everyone."

"Lorenzo, she loves you. She wanted me to pass on those very words, and she misses you and to look after yourself."

"Ah, that means so much to me. I'm sorry I can't invite you in."

"I know, mate, don't worry. I've just left you some food Eva made for you."

"Please thank her. I've had to freeze a lot, but I am grateful for her kindness."

"How is it going with the vaccination?"

"Good, we are starting on the 27 December. I've sorted out the venues. I'm just training staff. All is beginning to look hopeful at last."

"That is great news. Well, I'd better get on. You take care and we'll see you soon."

"Si, love to everyone. Ciao, John."

Brother Emmanuel's Death

(Morte di Fratello Emmanuel)

John had decided to close down the bread stall for the morning. Most people had collected their orders early and returned to the safety of their apartments.

He loaded the little van and headed up the Corsa Italia towards the monastery. Strangely, he welcomed the empty streets. He remembered the day last year when he had first arrived in Sorrento and had walked down this road at the height of a vicious thunderstorm. He had become soaked very quickly, and the pavements were full of squashed oranges, which the wind had ripped from the trees. He smiled as he recalled his feelings of anger and disillusionment when he realised his leather business in London was on the verge of bankruptcy after his business meeting in Naples had turned out to be a scam. And then he met Martha, a woman who he grew to admire and respect and one who had thrown him a lifeline.

What a year last year had been; it had been challenging for all of them to get the restaurant up and running. His constant battle with PTSD to keep his life on an even keel had been hard work. Everyone had helped him in different ways. Mary had listened to him and intuitively knew when he was having a bad day. She encouraged him with her practical, down-to-earth approach to dealing with his fears. Samantha also helped by showing him deep breathing exercises and how to show kindness to himself. Eva had cooked him his favourite foods, demonstrating to him that love could be simple but meaningful. Of course, the day Alfie came into his life, he realised he had much love to give and wasn't alone anymore.

He entered the driveway to the monastery, his last stop of the morning, and was struck by the silence of this godly world.

He pulled at the bell and listened as it resonated around the building. The echo was empty, like the monks had abandoned their faith and run away. Leaving the basket of bread by the old oak door, he wandered around the back of the building, looking for signs of life. He was trying to avoid the small cemetery, but, as usual, he was drawn towards it.

His heart sank down to his feet. Brother Emmanuel lay across Giovanni's grave. Two other brethren were by his side. Their agitation was evident.

John rushed over.

"Dio mio, (oh my God), che c'e? (What is wrong?) che c'e?

"E frate emanuele (It is Brother Emmanuel). Lui e morto (he is dead).

John stared into the face of the elderly monk. His mouth was gaping open in horror, and John knew his end had been far from peaceful. Kneeling down, he gently closed Emmanuel's eyes. The old monk must be in his nineties, and John thought his heart had probably failed him. But why had he died on Giovanni's grave of all places? He remembered Martha telling him about her conversation with the kind monk about his fear of Giovanni. Maybe he felt, as he sometimes did, the dark aura of the young man, even though he was dead, still managing to get a hold of people. With COVID and the stress it had inflicted on the world, particularly Italy, maybe Emmanuel had let his fears take over, and his heart had given way.

The Abbot came quickly on the scene. "The doctor is on his way to certify the death."

"I'll stay and help you move Emmanuel into the monastery. It is such a sad day. Please accept my condolences, Father. He was a very kind man and will be sincerely missed."

"Thank you, John. He was a much-loved brother and very well liked in the community. It is indeed a great loss to us." Tears began to well up in the Abbott's eyes. Emmanuel was like his brother. They had been together for so long, and the shock of his passing was beginning to hit him.

John carried the frail body of Emmanuel and laid him carefully on the simple bed in his room. He left the monastery with a heavy heart to return home with the bad news.

As he entered The Villa by the terraced gardens, Martha immediately greeted him.

"Hello, John, we were wondering where you were. Is everything all right? You look a bit frazzled."

"I've come from the monastery. I'm afraid I have some sad news. Brother Emmanuel has passed away."

"Oh no, John, that is awful." Martha instinctively clutched her throat. "He was only here last week. What happened?"

"It looks like his heart gave way. He was tending the graves when he collapsed."

"Really, tending the graves? You don't mean Giovanni's, do you? I tried to suggest he should keep away as I knew mentally he was struggling. He really felt he was being haunted by him."

"Yes, I'm afraid he was lying stretched over it. Oh dear, the lockdown has got us all a bit jittery.

Martha paused for a moment.

"Come walk with me, John. "There is something I should tell you. It's about when my father shot Hoffman, and we buried him in the monastery graveyard?

"Yes, of course, I remember you telling me."

"Some time ago, Brother Emmanuel confided in me about the war. He was here at the age of 14 as a novice after his family had been killed in the bombing of Napoli. The Germans had taken over the monastery and were very cruel to the monks. In particular, Hoffman was a sadist." Martha hesitated, not wanting to break a confidence, "Emmanuel saw us bury the Nazi, and this is hard to believe, but where we buried him is precisely the same grave where Giovanni is buried."

"You mean one on top of the other?" John's face showed his bewilderment.

"Yes, indeed," Martha replied.

"What! My goodness, that explains a lot. No wonder he felt all that evil. It must have always played on his heart, wearing him down."

"There is more, John; Poor Emmanuel was not only terrified of Hoffman but he was sexually abused by him when he was a young boy and in the place where he worshipped God. Obviously, the repercussions have stayed with him all of his life. When he saw us burying the Capitan, he was relieved he was dead, but the guilt stayed with him. Recently, the appearance of Giovanni has been making him question his faith and inability to forgive."

"The poor man. He must have suffered greatly. It is this kind of thing that makes my blood boil. How can people be so cruel to each other?

"I agree, John. Poor Emmanuel, I will miss him. He was quite a character, and he loved visiting The Villa. I'll ring the Abbot later to offer my condolences. The local people will be upset to hear he has passed. He was very much respected in this area. It's all so sad."

"I find it very odd, Martha. I'm not religious and don't believe in an after life, but now I'm beginning to wonder. There is definitely a strange atmosphere in the monastery graveyard. I hope they bury him well away from Giovanni and Hoffman."

"I'm inclined to agree with you, John. I may speak with the Abbot and tell him how Brother Emmanuel confided in me about his fear of Giovanni, and perhaps a resting place nearer the monastery itself would have been what he wanted. It's worth a try. Shall we head back? It's past lunchtime. You must be hungry."

John took Martha's arm, and together, they walked back to The Villa, both engrossed in their thoughts.

Martha's Plan

(Il Piano di Martha)

2020 was nearing its end. It had been a testing year. They had survived the terror and fear of illness. However, like everyone who had experienced the pandemic, the anxiety remained below the surface, ready to spring back to life at any moment to disrupt their world again.

There was no time for complacency or relaxation. The number of people infected with COVID-19 increased, and distancing and facemasks were again part of everyday life. The good news was that the vaccine would be rolled out on 27 December to healthcare workers and the vulnerable. From February 2021, the entire population would have the opportunity to be vaccinated. In the meantime, life continued as normal as possible.

Martha was looking for John. She was anxious to speak to him. "Have you seen John? She asked Sam who was nursing her baby and chatting to Henrik and Eva in the kitchen.

"He's in the wine cellar. The new tables and chairs have arrived, and he's setting them up. He said he doesn't want anyone to go in until he has finished." Henrik said.

"I'm sure he won't mind if I have a quick word with him." Martha said as she set off across the courtyard. Her mind was full of the conversation she had just had with the Abbott.

"John, are you there?" she called as she entered the cellar.

Alfie came rushing out, barking loudly and quickly, followed by John.

"Hello Martha, did you want me?"

"Yes, dear, I won't keep you. I can see you are busy."

"Come in and have a quick preview. Tell me honestly what you think. I'm rather pleased with the new furniture."

Martha looked around at the newly created cellar. John had arranged the bistro-style table and chairs in groups. The black wrought iron furniture was complimented by coffee-coloured cushions and blended nicely with the creamy stonewalls.

"I've spoken to Chloe, and she will supply us with a selection of French cheeses to sell. She is making plans to open her shop when the time is right. What do you think, Martha? Tell me honestly?"

"It's perfect, John," she replied. "It looks very French. I like the burned-down candles in the old dusty wine bottles. It gives it a lovely nostalgic feel. And I think the lighting is just right. I hope it won't be long before we can welcome guests."

"So do I, Martha. We are in a waiting game before we can get back to normal. At least we will be prepared. I was thinking a variety of wines in the racks over there." He pointed to the wooden shelving. Signor Miccio will help me source them."

Martha smiled. "He is the right man for the job and will be thrilled to help. I'm sure we will get there eventually. Hopefully, next season will be better. Anyway, John, I need to talk to you. The Abbot has telephoned to say Brother Emmanuel will be buried on Sunday at 2 p.m. I asked if he minded if we attended, and he insisted we should.

He also said they had chosen a prominent place under the wooden cross at the head of the main burial ground."

"Well, that is very fitting. He deserves to have pride of place. He was very much loved by the community and dedicated his life to God. Would you like me to go with you, Martha? I think I would like to pay my respects."

"Of course I would love you to. The thing is, John, I'd like your opinion on an idea that suddenly came to me in the middle of the night. Why not bury the jewelled sword with Brother Emmanuel? This will protect him from evil spirits, and we won't have to hide it anymore."

"But Martha, it could be worth millions. We don't have the right to do that."

"I agree partly with you, John. We assume it has come from a great cathedral, but doesn't that poor man who suffered terrible abuse at such a tender age from the Nazis deserve full honours. He was a kind, genuine man who dedicated his life to others and, besides my father, spent many years of anxiety and worry about something precious hidden here in the cellar. He knew if it was discovered, he would be imprisoned or worse killed, and it wasn't his fault."

John hesitated for a moment. He couldn't decide if this was a criminal act or a solution to a thorny problem. "I'm not sure, Martha. How would we get it in the coffin without the other monks seeing it?"

"I've thought about that. I wonder if you could make a cover out of some old pieces of wood so the sword looks more like a wooden cross? No one would know there was a precious object hidden within it. We could say Emmanuel had always admired the cross in The Villa, and we would like him to take it on his new journey to protect him."

John laughed. "Martha, you are amazing. No one else would have thought of that."

"I must get it from my father. After all, he had successfully hidden the sword for many years. It is time to bury it forever, and I love the idea. We can then stop worrying about it."

"I agree. I'll take some measurements and

make a very fitting cover for it. I have some bits of olive wood that would do the trick."

"Thank you, John. I knew you would approve."

"How could I not, Martha. You are very convincing." He smiled and held her arm as they returned to the house.

Later that evening, John went to his workshed. He laid the ornate sword on his bench and studied the workmanship. He couldn't believe he was looking at an artefact of such historical value. His knowledge of gemstones was limited. After taking a photograph, he decided to Google the history of the Nazi's involvement in stealing the most precious works of art. Many famous paintings were missing around the world. Maybe someone at this very moment was looking at a Rembrandt or a Michelangelo sculpture in their private art gallery. Surely, Martha's suggestion was the right thing to do. This was a religious piece and shouldn't be owned by some wealthy person. He could see twelve very prevalent rubies, sapphires, and emeralds adorning the sword, and he further discovered that these might have represented the 12 Apostles. His research on the Internet led him to believe that this could be early Christian or medieval art.

John's mind wandered back to Brother Emmanuel. He was a simple soul whose life had been difficult, and John was convinced that laying the sword in the arms of such a kind, genuine person was a fitting end. After all, it was only a man-made objet d'art, and slaves would probably have been used to hew out these precious stones in Roman times, causing much suffering to them physically and mentally.

He remembered the look of horror on the poor monk's face, and John had realised that some evil force had mentally tortured this man, and his death had been far from peaceful. Maybe it was all in his head, but John knew how that felt. Many times during his life in Afghanistan, he had been scared, and his compassion for the old monk had helped him make up his mind to agree that it was a fitting-resting place for the sword.

He quickly searched through his scraps of wood and found the perfect piece. It was a dark nutmeg colour. He had to use all his skills to create a shield to disguise the hidden sword. He realised they had to be careful that the Abbot didn't pick up the piece, which was tremendously heavy, and he may question why. John chose a particularly gnarled section that looked like the shape of the Madonna in prayer. Working slowly, he managed to glue the pieces, and a genuine-looking religious cross emerged before his eyes. Rubbing his fingers over the tactile and sensuous fibres, he marvelled at the depth of grain. He felt he had created something exceptional and couldn't wait to see Martha's reaction.

***

A few days later, they both stood in the small, cold Sacristy. Brother Emmanuel was laid out in his open coffin. The dark room was lit with candles, and the chants from the monks as they made their way to prayer added a sense of solemnity to the occasion. Peace and tranquillity filled the room. Martha and John stood silently as they gazed at the parchment skin covering Emmanuel's face like a veil. His soul had clearly left him, and all that remained was the symbolic 'overcoat' of his body, ready to be buried forever.

The Abbot had permitted Martha to place the cross in the coffin with Emmanuel. Allowing them a few moments of privacy while they did this, he thanked God for their compassion for his dear friend. With John's help, the sword was now firmly placed in the arms of Brother Emmanuel. From the outside world, it resembled an ancient cross. This kind, elderly man was being honoured in an extraordinary way.

The service was simple, and Martha had to hold back the tears as the coffin was lowered into the ground. Even John was standing straight, trying to compose his thoughts. He had seen many burials, but this one seemed particularly poignant.

John glanced around as they both walked back to the car. He was comforted by the thought that Brother Emmanuel was well away from the cruel Nazi and Guiseppe. John felt an overwhelming sense of calm that the sacred sword would guide Emmanuel on his travels to the next life. He took Martha's arm and gently helped her down the steep slope.

'I feel we have done the right thing, Martha. Come on, it's time to go home."

Surprise Wedding
(Matrimonio a Sorpresa)

Christmas was a month away, and everyone in The Villa wondered how to make it memorable. The kitchen was the meeting point to get together to make plans.

The idea of spending Christmas day with a traditional meal and presents around the tree was immediately met with enthusiasm, especially as Coronavirus restrictions were expected to be reintroduced. Samantha had also put forward a suggestion for those who wanted to join her in a small candle-lit remembrance party in the cove later in the evening. She suggested a spiritual theme to give thanks for the year's survival from COVID-19 and as a symbol of hope for the future. This was Robbie's resting place, but it was also the birthplace of her daughter, and she wanted to do something special.

Everyone was enthusiastic about the idea. Henrik took Eva's arm and led her to one side.

"Eva, I'm not sure how you feel about this, but I

want to marry you now."

"What! You mean right now in this moment."

"No, I want to marry you at the cove on Christmas Eve. Like Samantha said, it is a special place."

"But we can't. First of all, it's Mary and my father's anniversary, and secondly, your parents and family are in Denmark."

"Yes, I know, but we don't know how long the restrictions will continue with the virus. It could be many months. It may be ages before my family can travel. Anyway, we can always have a blessing in Copenhagen when the time is right. But right now, I want you. I need you. I want to be your husband and to love you forever."

Eva didn't hesitate. She threw her arms around him, yelling, "Yes, it's a brilliant idea, but maybe make it New Year's Eve. Then, we will start the New Year as husband and wife, and we won't be intruding on everyone else's celebrations. What do you think?"

"I like it. Let's tell the others and see what they say?"

She looked into his eyes and kissed him passionately on the lips. He immediately cupped her face in his hands and kissed her back.

The news was met with renewed excitement.

"What a lovely idea," Samantha said.

Eva turned to her father and Mary.

"How do you guys feel about another family wedding at The Villa?"

Franco looked at Mary.

They both burst out laughing. "Are you kidding? This is the best news ever."

"Well, this is exciting," Martha, said. "Have you any idea what kind of ceremony it would be?"

Henrik turned to Eva. "Unless you have something special in mind, I would like to arrange the wedding as a surprise for you. I think you will be pleased with what I have planned."

"You mean you are going to organise everything?" she asked.

"Yes, everything, including your dress and, especially, the food. You will not be cooking on your wedding day."

"Eva, dear, you looked shocked," Martha said as she motioned to a chair. "Come and sit down next to me."

Eva sat down. She was lost for words.

Henrik continued. "The only help I will need is that of the gentlemen in the room."

"You can count on us, Henrik," John said. "I'm looking forward to it, just as long as you don't want me cooking in the kitchen."

"But, we will be involved, surely," said Mary.

"I would like to keep it a surprise for the ladies also, but I may need your advice on one or two things, which I will ask later. I will update you with dates and times via the kitchen notice board and requests for secret meetings if I need help."

"It does sound like fun. I think I like the idea of a surprise wedding." She smiled at Henrik. "It's so romantic. I love it."

***

Later that afternoon, Henrik headed down to the cove. John and Franco had agreed to meet him there to discuss his plans. His sudden outburst of announcing to Eva that he would arrange the wedding himself was now uppermost in his mind, and he wanted to start planning as he had an idea of what kind of wedding to organise. There was no way he was going to let her down.

He headed straight for the boathouse, which had been part of The Villa since it was built many years ago. It had a wooden structure, and age had been kind to it, giving it a soft, rustic look. Inside, it was very dry. The floor was made from wooden planks, and oversized windows let in a lot of hazy sunlight. Henrik was drawn towards a large rowing boat lying at an angle against the wall. He ran his hands over the gunwale. It was smooth, and it felt good to be alone with a boat again. Fishing and boating had been a natural pastime in Denmark for Henrik. When Franco asked if he wanted to help renovate his lugger boat, Henrik had agreed in a flash. His dream was to own his own boat one day. At the moment, he was wondering how to achieve his idea of creating a Viking wedding for his bride. In his mind, he could envisage Eva walking with her guests down to the boathouse, her long dress trailing in the breeze. As she waited for him in the sunset hours, he would sail into the cove on his Viking ship wearing a traditional Danish costume, ready to marry his woman. The only problem was turning the old rowing boat into a Viking ship!

Alfie arrived first, with John following at a slower pace. Franco came in from the cove entrance in his small motorboat five minutes later. He tied the boat to a post and waded through the clear water to join them.

"Hej, herovre" (hello, over here), Henrik yelled. He'd forgotten he was in Italy and not Denmark; his head was full of Danish nostalgia.

Franco replied with a wave and a "Hej."

"Thanks so much for coming. It's really good of you to give up your time. I wanted to share my ideas about the wedding and hope you have some thoughts.

"Brilliant," John said. He noticed the boathouse door was open. "Shall we go and sit down inside. I've bought some paper and pen to jot down notes and a few bottles of beer."

"Yes, come on in, guys," Henrik replied. "I'll

explain what I have in mind. As a proud Danish man, I want to include my heritage in the wedding. So I thought, why not have a Viking wedding?"

"Great idea," John replied instantly.

And Franco immediately agreed. "Eva will love it."

"I'm going to ask my parents to help, although I don't think they will be able to get a flight over, with the restrictions as they are. But I'm hoping Mum will sort out the clothes. I am thinking that this boathouse could be turned into a Viking hut. Perhaps a fire pit or two to keep it warm, and maybe bring the wooden table and chairs in from The Villa for the food celebration." Henrik gulped for air, excited by all the ideas floating through his head.

"I would love a Viking ship to come into the cove, and if Martha doesn't mind, I thought we could redesign her old wooden boat. I don't know if it's possible, but could we rig up some kind of dragon's head at the bow and maybe some false oars at the side? It would also need a square sail with some sort of design on it. I'm not sure yet. Eva will be waiting down here after a traditional walk from the house to her wedding with her female guests. In Denmark, the tradition is that the male guests lead the groom, or drag him, to his bride."

John looked around the boathouse. The rowing boat caught his eye, and he went over to it. "I think we could do something with this. The wood is still good and can easily be turned into a Viking vessel. I'm sure Franco and I can turn you into a proud Viking. After all, he has refurbished his lugger boat, so he knows what he is doing."

"It would be an honour, Henrik. You are marrying my daughter, and only the best is good enough, and a Viking wedding sounds perfect." Franco agreed.

"Thanks, guys. I knew I could rely on you. The more I think about it, the more I know it will work. I'll make a plan of what is involved. I will need a lot of fur to cover the wooden chairs and for costumes. I can't imagine there is anywhere in Italy that would sell it.

"Of course there is. We have an Ikea store in Afragola in Naples. They may be able to deliver what you need." Franco said.

"That would be amazing. We must have fur; it's part of the tradition. Also, foodwise, I need to think about a pig roast and lots of fish.

"I may know someone who can help you with the fish." John winked at Franco. "Let's drink beer and get into the Viking spirit. We can toast the future bride and groom."

***

Later that evening, Henrik slipped away to have a quiet Zoom call with his parents.

"Hej mor og far (hi, mum and dad). I have some news to tell you, and I hope you won't be too disappointed."

"Hej Henrik skat (hello, Henrik darling). We hope it is good news. We've already had to cancel our trip to see you, as the flights will not be going to Italy yet. We have another wave of Coronavirus."

"Yes, I thought that would happen. It is the same over here. There is little air traffic. I wanted to tell you something, and I hope you don't mind, but I want to marry Eva now. We have no idea when we can come to Denmark to get married; it could be another year. However, we plan on getting married on New Year's Eve in a quiet ceremony here at The Villa. We would like a big celebration at home when everything is normal. What do you think?"

Henrik's parents looked at each other. He could tell by their expression they were disappointed.

"Look," he said, "I will set up a video link so you can see the proceedings and be part of it. I would love you to be here, but it's been such a challenging year, and we both want to be together. I want to involve you in the arrangements and need your help."

"Of course, we understand. We were in love once." His mother replied as she squeezed her husband's hand.

"We still are," chipped in his father. "What have

you in mind, son and how can we help?"

"I'm organising everything, and I've told Eva she doesn't have to do a thing, no preparing or cooking. It will be a total surprise. What I am planning is a Viking Wedding. There is a little cove with a boathouse as part of The Villa. I've asked all the men to help me, and I intend to recreate a Viking hut with wooden tables and chairs, candles and tankards, etc. I'm going to prepare a traditional feast. We have a rustic old boat; with John and Franco's help, we plan to turn it into a Viking ship. It all sounds a bit silly, but it will be fun."

"It sounds wonderful, darling. How can I help you?"

"Well, Mum, I need your advice on a Viking Wedding dress. Where could I buy the costume from and have them deliver it here? I need a costume for me as well? Also, I need the family recipe for a wedding cake? And anything else you can think of to make it traditional."

"OK, I can help with that. I'll get on to it straight away. There are only a few weeks, but there will be time. It does sound very exciting and such a lot of fun. Your father and I will be glued to our computer. It's such a shame we can't be there."

"Look, Mum, if things change and there is any chance you can come, we will aim for that. I love you both very much."

"Henrik, darling, we have all gone through a worrying ordeal, and I think an excuse to celebrate and have fun must be taken. We don't know what the future holds for any of us. So go ahead and have a wonderful time. We will certainly be with you even if it's on Zoom." She laughed. "Let me know Eva's measurements, and I will happily find a dress for her."

"Thanks, both of you. I'll be in touch soon. Farvel (goodbye)."

"Farvel, Henrik. Kys kys (kiss, kiss)"

Henrik's Plan

(Il Piano Di Henrik)

Franco was preparing for a night's fishing.

"Are you sure you want to come tonight, Maria? It will be quite cool on the water."

"Of course, I want to help you. With these new restrictions being imposed, we will have to return to delivering the fish ourselves. It makes you wonder if life will ever be normal again."

"I know it is disappointing, but they did warn us that it could return again in the winter. Its shame Henrik's parents have had to cancel their trip. I can't see air travel being possible over Christmas and the New Year."

"I think it's going to be a small wedding, but I'm sure it will be lovely," Mary said as she put her arms around her husband. "So, you were going to tell me about the plans. What kind of wedding has Henrik in mind?"

"Aspettare (hold on), I'm sworn to secrecy. There is no way I'm telling you or any of the women what is happening, and I am surprised at you for asking me."

"But I'm your wife. We have no secrets, and I promise I won't tell anybody. In fact, I may be able to help with the arrangements." She ran her fingers through his hair and moved closer, her lips brushing his cheek.

"Stop that. Maria, you cannot get around me. It is not fair to ask me." Franco said as he tried to move away.

She decided to change tactics. "Come on then, the fish won't wait forever." She moved towards the door, and a smile of anticipation crept over her face. One way or another, she was determined to get the secret out of him.

***

A few days later, Henrik and John stood in the boat shed. They were leaning over a large drawing of a rowing boat. Martha had been delighted to give them her old boat to do with whatever they needed.

"I think it may be possible to turn this old wreck into a magnificent Viking ship," Franco said.

"What do you think, John?"

"I've done some things in my life, but never anything like this. I'm really up for the challenge."

Franco's phone went off loudly. "Pronto," he said, followed by a long, animated conversation with the person on the other end.

"Good news. That was Nello from Castellamare boatyard. He can let us have eight old oars. No charge. He's going to drop them off later today."

"Wow, that's brilliant."

"He's quite a character. Such a big, strong man but has a heart of gold. When I explained you were organising a secret wedding, he couldn't wait to help. I think he must be a romantic at heart."

Henrik smiled. "I hope we can have guests join us for the wedding. Nello will certainly be on the list."

"It shouldn't be difficult to insert the oars into the side of the boat. I also need to put in a small engine, but that shouldn't be a problem. What about the figurehead?" Franco said.

"It is customary to have a dragon's head. They were to frighten the enemy or ward off evil monsters from the sea."

"Don't let Mary hear you say that. She'll want one for our fishing boat. I've seen the look on her face when there is a weird fish in the nets." Franco laughed.

"I've got some really large pieces of wood. I could hollow them out and try and make something. Would that work, do you think?" John said.

"Yes, that sounds brilliant. We can paint it. It's really only for effect from a distance. Just to add a bit of fun."

"Good, I'll get on to that straight away. What else do you need?"

"A large fire pit."

"Is this for cooking or warmth?"

"Definitely to keep everyone warm. It will be cold, and the ceremony will be at sunset so the temperature will drop. I'm waiting for the Celebrant to confirm if that time is possible."

"So you will need a pile of logs. I'll check the

log store. I may have to cut down some trees." John added this to his notebook.

"Talking of trees, I hoped to have a few Christmas trees dotted around the boatshed. Would that be possible?"

"It's not a problem at all. We can get some from Monte Faito or the hills above The Villa. I think it's going to look great. We will also need to bring the wooden table and chairs from the restaurant. The best way would be to bring them in by boat into the cove." Franco was really getting into the spirit of the preparations for his daughter's big day.

"Did you say you wanted to do a pig roast, Henrik? If so, we can also bring the roasting spit from the restaurant down here by boat." John said.

"Yes, that would be great. Now, regarding clothes. My mother is organising Eva's wedding dress and is looking at hiring costumes for the men. I wanted to surprise the ladies, but they will need to decide what to wear. Do you think we should ask Mary to help regarding this?"

"I think that would be a good idea," Franco said. "You have no idea the lengths she has been going to to get information out of me. I have seen a different side to her and I'm not sure I like it."

John laughed. "I think we can imagine what you are going through."

"Well, I think that's it for now. There is such a lot to do. Thanks guys for helping me. I couldn't do it without you." Henrik smiled his appreciation was evident.

"No need for thanks. We are looking forward to it, aren't we, John."

"Indeed, I can't wait to get my hands on some wood and do a bit of carving. One thing, Henrik, remember I've got the machinery from my leather business. I could make some leather jerkins and belts for costumes, and if we can get some sheepskin from Ikea, we can recreate a Danish look for the 'Viking men.'

"Tak gutter (thanks, guys). That would be great. It means such a lot to me."

***

Mary was in the kitchen. She had delivered some fresh fish for Eva and was chatting with Samantha.

"Have you any clues as to what Henrik is organising for the wedding?" she asked Sam. "Franco refuses to tell me anything despite all my efforts to make him talk."

"Poor Franco, I bet you are making his life a misery."

"On the contrary. I am spoiling him with love and affection. Not to mention his favourite foods. But he is so stubborn he just won't give in. "Mary laughed." I even sat on him the other night and tickled him, and I refused to get off until he told me, but he just closed his eyes and nodded off."

"Maybe that envelope on the notice board addressed to you could be a secret message from my fiancée," Eva said.

Mary rushed over and grabbed the letter. She ripped it open and said. "He wants to see me at 2 o'clock in John's workshop. Oh, I can't stand surprises. I need to know what is going off."

"Mary, surprises are brilliant fun. I love the

mystery of it all."

"But, there is so much to organise? What are we all going to wear for a start? We need time to plan."

"I agree with Eva," Samantha said. "I'm sure we will find out bits and pieces. Maybe Henrik wants to ask your advice."

"Well, it's nearly time to go there and find out. Do you want me to tell you?"

"No," They both shouted together.

***

Henrik was busy in John's workshop cutting out material to make costumes, when Mary knocked at the door. He quickly glanced around to make sure everything was hidden from sight.

"I'm coming," he yelled.

"Hi," Mary said. "You wanted a word? How can I help?"

"Ciao, come in. I've started planning the ceremony, and I don't want to spoil the surprise for Eva and everybody so I'm hoping you can help me with something without giving it away."

"Of course, Henrik. I wouldn't dream of spoiling the surprise. You can count on me." Mary moved closer, eager to hear more.

"I have Eva's wedding dress under control, but for the guests, especially the ladies, it would be good if they could wear long simple gowns, mainly creams, coffee colours, pale blues. I will provide additional items to add to their dresses, and they will hopefully be delighted on the day. So would you mind asking Sam and Martha if they agree?"

"Yes, of course I will," Mary, said. "What about Signor Miccio? What would he be wearing?"

"Don't worry about that. He is already part of the organising team. He knows exactly what he has to wear."

Mary sighed. She knew she wasn't going to get any information from Henrik. She may need to use her charms on Signor Miccio.

"Well, if there is anything else, let me know." She walked away, even more intrigued and frustrated.

"I will, Mary, and thank you."

The Heat Is On
(Il Riscaldamento e acceso)

The days before Christmas were extremely busy, and the pressure was building, especially for Henrik. He was settled in John's work shed and was looking at his 'to-do' list. His biggest challenge had been turning the old boat into a mini Viking ship, and that had been achieved with brilliant success. He knew exactly what he was doing regarding the food and cake. The Celebrant had confirmed his availability on New Year's Eve, and the time had been arranged for 4.30 p.m. just as the sun would be setting. Henrik had written his vows, which had become a love story in poetry.

"Gosh, I must tell Eva about writing her vows, too." He added it to his list. The furniture they would use was to be brought around on Franco's boat. That was a job for the day before the wedding. Franco and John had volunteered to help him do this and decorate the boathouse with garlands of flowers and a traditional Viking arch made out of tree bark for the bride and groom to stand under for the ceremony. He had ordered the wedding rings online, and to his delight, they had arrived on time. He had chosen a wedding band made of twisted white gold with tiny diamonds for Eva and plain for him. They were exactly what he wanted, and felt sure she would be delighted.

A knock at the door made him jump. He quickly hid his notes and rushed to open the door. Mary stood there clutching a large cardboard box.

"A delivery for you, Henrik. I thought it looked important, so I've brought it over."

"Oh, Mary. It's from my mother. Thank goodness it has arrived. I was beginning to panic."

"Do you need a hand with it?"

"No, thank you. I can manage."

A little disappointed, she turned to walk away.

"Mary, there is something I need to ask you. Are the ladies happy with wearing a plain long dress? I know it is an odd request, but it will all make sense on the day."

Mary smiled. "They were puzzled, but we have sorted out dresses that are not too fussy. Martha is in a pale blue long-sleeved silk number. I'm in my wedding dress, although I have taken the lace-over dress off, and Samantha is wearing an olive green long cotton dress."

"Awesome," Henrik smiled. "You know, I think it is all going to be all right."

"Well, don't forget, I'm here and ready and willing to help."

"Thank you, I'll remember that."

As soon as Mary had gone, Henrik locked the door and opened the box. He felt nervous. What if Eva's dress wasn't right or didn't fit? He needn't have worried as he removed the tissue paper to reveal a perfect replica of a Viking bride's dress. It was rich, heavy brocade in deep red the traditional colour for a Viking bride. It's long tight sleeves were edged with criss cross ties and pointed cuffs in an embroidered lighter red colour and the same around the neck and hem of the skirt. It was beautifully made with a tight bodice and a very full skirt. To add the finishing touches, a fur wrap completed the Viking look. Henrik's mother also included a range of heavy metal necklaces, glittery hair bands, faux fur stoles, and leather gloves.

He delved a bit deeper into the box to discover his own outfit. It consisted of a long leather coat in sage green with dark coffee-coloured elbow-length leather bracers criss crossed with heavy straps and buckles. The look was completed with a pair of dark green suede trousers, a fur shoulder wrap, and a Viking helmet and sword.

Henrik immediately phoned his mother.

"The parcel has arrived, and the dress is perfect. I'm sure she will love it, mor (mum). Thank you so much, and I love my outfit. I can't wait to try it on."

"I hope it all fits. How are the arrangements going?"

"It's going very well. Of course, the food will be the next big thing. Everyone is excited, and I've kept it all a surprise."

"You mean Eva doesn't know it is a Viking wedding."

"No, she has no idea, but she is aware it is a bit quirky, and she thinks it's all very romantic and can't wait to marry me."

"I am sure it will be wonderful, and your father and I have accepted that we can't be with you, but we will be watching on the video link and, just so we don't miss out, we will also be wearing Viking attire."

Henrik laughed. "Just brilliant, mum. Honestly, we will have another celebration when it is safe to fly. I promise."

"I know, sweetheart. It's just how things are, but we will be with you in spirit. Take care. Speak soon."

"Bye, mum, love you."

"Bye, Henrik, my Viking Warrior. I love you too."

A few moments later, John came into the workshop. "Mary said you've received a mystery parcel. I guess it's Eva's wedding dress."

"Hi John, come and look. What do you think of

this?" He held up the stunning red dress.

"Wow, she is going to look fabulous, especially with her dark hair, and look at the fur cloak. It's gorgeous. We need to sort out what the guys will be wearing."

"Mum said for the men, all they need is baggy white shirts and loose cotton trousers. Maybe leather waistcoats. We should be able to make some fun costumes from these bits and pieces she has sent."

"We can manage it, Henrik. I've got lots of pieces of leather in my workshed and can make some loose jerkins for the men. It shouldn't be too difficult. What would look good is some kind of armoury like gauntlets or straps and things. You know, with the cheap fur rugs we've bought, we have everything we need for cloaks. How are we with the ladies' costumes? Should we ask Mary for her help?

"Yes, I've already spoken to Mary, so that part is organised, although she knows very little. Regarding the boat, I'm really pleased with the progress so far. Franco has already attached the oars to give an impression of a ship."

"Well," John said. "Let me show you what I've been working on. Take a look at this." John reached for a huge blanket lying on the floor and revealed his attempt at making a Viking figurehead.

"Wow, I don't know what to say. It's amazing." Henrik stroked the head of the wooden dragon.

"It needs a bit of paint on the eyes to bring it to life. I'm really pleased with it. Franco is coming tomorrow morning, and we will attach it to the boat."

"I'll help you carry it down there."

"Is there much more for you to do, Henrik?"

"I have the cake to make, but I can't do that until just before the wedding. It's a traditional wedding cake called 'Kransekage'. I've never made one before, but mum has sent the recipe and the metal rings to make it. It's relatively easy. It's made of almond-flavoured dough made with eggs and sugar, and it is shaped like a cone with sections made into rings. It denotes wedding rings and is a beautiful delicacy but the texture is like a biscuit and the flavour is maple and almond or indeed, whatever you want. I may do some lemon flavoured ones, as Eva adores lemons."

"It sounds delicious. I can't wait. In fact, I'm really looking forward to dressing up as a Viking. It's such a shame your parents can't come."

"I know, but they are resigned to the fact they can't be here, but they are happy Eva and I are getting married, and we will have a big celebration in Denmark for the family as soon as we can travel. In fact, Mum is already making plans. That reminds me, I need to set up a video link so they can be included in the day."

"Sorry, Henrik, I can't help you there. My talents lie solely with bits of leather and sewing! Technology is a foreign language to me."

"I can do it. Thanks, John, for all your help. I can't tell you what it means to me."

"That's OK, old chap," John said as he patted him on the shoulder. He wasn't used to compliments, but it did make him feel good.

Christmas Day

(Giorno di Natale)

Christmas day began early for John, who was up before everyone else and was taking Alfie for his morning walk. They headed down to the cove, and the boat shed. It was quiet and peaceful, an emotion that John had felt very strongly during this year of Covid. Feeling calm for the first time in years, his eyes rested on the Viking boat, and he couldn't help but smile. It was such a wonderful romantic idea, and he had to admit the boat, even though a little comical, was pretty good.

"Look at that dragon, Alfie. I made that." Alfie looked at John and then growled at the dragon's head. "Yes," thought John. 'Even Alfie believes it is real, so it must be good.'

He sat down with his dog on his lap and reflected on the last year. He thought about Chloe. He really liked her, she had attitude, but also a kind heart, and he hoped to get to know her better. Sadly, Covid had put this on hold. They had spoken a lot on the phone, and he felt she liked him. He looked forward to getting to know her more as soon as this wretched virus was over.

He stroked his little dog and wondered what kind of life Alfie had had before he had come into their lives.

"Was someone cruel to you, mate?" He asked. Alfie looked up with sadness in his eyes. "Never mind, I have you now and will always look after you. You are number one in my life, and don't ever doubt it."

They sat together quietly, John reflecting on the past and the future for them both. Alfie just nestled next to him, content in his own world. He was a very happy dog.

After an hour of peaceful contemplation, John locked the boathouse, and they made their way outside. A fantastic golden light was shining on the water. It stopped John in his tracks, and he stared as though mesmerised by something ethereal. The light rippled across the calm water and danced at his feet. It felt supernatural, as though someone was trying to reaffirm his positive thoughts.

"My God, it must be Robbie," he said to Alfie, who was mesmerised by the light surrounding his body and was playfully moving around. They watched as the golden rays flickered over them and silently disappeared into the calm water.

For the first time in John's life, he felt like a spirit had touched him. It was Christmas Day, and something extraordinary had just happened to him. He walked slowly back up the track, thankful that he and his dog were alive and well and open to a beautiful future ahead of them.

***

Christmas lunch was a very relaxed affair with all the trimmings, including traditional English and Italian food, colourfully spread out on the long table. It was a happy occasion, especially as Lorenzo could join them. He was Covid free and had two days off work before the vaccination process started. The hugs he received were just what he needed, and he sank into the arms of the woman and child that filled his heart with joy.

"I am so glad you made it. Come in. We are just about to carve the turkey."

Lorenzo gently hugged his daughter closer to him.

"I have been longing for this moment, Samantha. Rosa looks so well and has grown since I last saw her."

"She is a bonny little thing," Mary said as she patted Lorenzo on the shoulder. "We have missed you. How are things out there in the world?"

"It is organised chaos. This virus is very challenging. All we can do is to keep a distance and pray the vaccine will work. I'm sure things will be much better this time next year."

"Lorenzo," Martha cried as she entered the room. "Come Vai?" (How are you?)" It is lovely that you are here for Christmas. We couldn't have asked for a better gift."

"Grazie, Signora. I couldn't keep away from you all, especially this little one." He held Rosa closer to him, and she, in return, stared at her father, and a smile burst over her face. "Did you see that? She smiled at me."

"Of course she did. She recognised her papa." Samantha said.

"Can I say something before we begin?" Martha said as she raised her glass. "I know it has been a challenging year, but I am so proud of you all for helping each other through it. I know it's not over yet, and we have more obstacles to overcome, but I want to wish you all a very happy Christmas."

Mary stood up. "I'd just like to add to that, Martha. We were celebrating our wedding a year ago today, and very soon, we will salute Eva and Henrik's marriage. On top of that, we have the addition of Rosa, Sam, and Lorenzo's beautiful daughter, who has come into our family to bring us all joy. "Salute e buona salute a tutti." Cheers and good health, everyone."

And so the party began. The fire crackling in the hearth filled the room with warmth, and the wood's pine fragrance added to the festive atmosphere. The twinkling lights on the tree and soft background music made a perfect happy Christmas day. Eventually, the conversation got round to Eva and Henrik's forthcoming wedding.

"I have to say," Mary said, as she helped herself to another spoonful of the delicious frozen citrus pudding, "despite all my attempts to find out what Henrik has planned for his surprise wedding, I am pleased I don't know. I am so excited. This is gorgeous, by the way." She said as she filled her dish with more dessert.

"So am I," Eva replied. "Although I am getting a little bit anxious. It's only six days away, and I haven't got a dress to wear!"

All eyes turned to Henrik, who just grinned back at them.

"Don't worry, everything will be revealed shortly. It is all booked, and I will post cryptic clues on the kitchen noticeboard starting today. All I need from you is to get into the spirit of the occasion, let your hair down, and enjoy yourselves."

"We can second that," John said. "As part of the wedding planning team, we gentlemen have done a sterling job organising this auspicious event. I think it will go down in history as a wedding to remember!"

"Now I am worried," Eva said.

"I think we all are," Mary laughed. "I can't imagine Franco organising a wedding."

"You will be surprised, my love. I have talents you are not yet aware of." Franco smiled. "My precious daughter will marry her true love in a very romantic way."

Martha interrupted. "I have every faith in you all, although I am a little worried about what I will be wearing."

"Your outfit has been designed and made with you in mind, Martha. Do not worry. You will love it?" Henrik said whilst leaning over to John and whispering in his ear. "You have done it, haven't you, John?"

"No, I thought you were doing it!"

Mary, listening to this exchange, looked at them both.

"I knew it! You've slipped up there. You really need my help. You can't let Eva down."

"It is just a slight hiccup, nothing we can't fix, is it Henrik?" John said.

Henrik, who was now pouring himself another large glass of wine, agreed.

"Yes, just a slight hiccup, everything's under control." He then signalled to John "Can you meet me later in the workshop we have work to do."

Final Touches
(Tocco Finale)

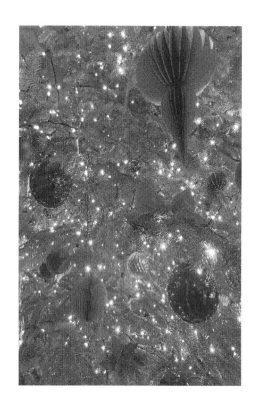

The 'Viking' men had performed an amazing feat. The boathouse had been turned into a magnificent venue for a traditional Nordic wedding. The long oak table and chairs had been carried down from The Villa and were decorated with large candelabras and black candles. Rich dark red and orange flowers mixed with trailing leaves draped over the table and wooden bowls filled with pomegranates, oranges and figs, from the trees, were placed in the centre of the table. Henrik had pinned to the wooden walls of the room large tree branches and entwined them with golden fairy lights. Pieces of faux fur were draped over the chairs, and an enormous red and brown carpet had been brought down from the attic to add warmth to the floor. A tall pine Christmas tree with simple golden twinkling lights stood in the corner.

Outside on the beach, a huge metal fire pit

was full of logs ready for the ceremony, and a spit was prepared and ready for the roasting of the pig.

On the sand and facing the gentle rippling water of the cove was a large ceremonial archway made from branches and anchored safely into the ground with spikes. Henrik had twisted red and orange flowers, trailing catkins and rich dark red berries into the wood, and at each side of the 'altar' were two large metal torch holders.

He stood back to admire his work.

"What do you think, guys? Is there anything missing?

"Yes," Signor Miccio said. "What about toilet facilities?"

"OMG, I hadn't thought of that."

"Don't worry, Henrik, I'll arrange something temporary." John said. "We used to do it in the army. It will be a wooden bench with a hole in it, and I'll dig a hole in the ground. I'm sure it will be ok for the short time we are here."

"Thanks, John. Gosh, that was something that hadn't occurred to me," he said laughing.

"I think also we need to bring down the two large throne chairs Martha has in the reception room. They'd be ideal for the bride and groom. The large wooden tree stumps are great for everyone else. We can throw some fur rugs on them." John said.

"We need something comfortable for Martha too. It's going to be a long time for her to sit. What about bringing the swing seat down? We can cover it with blankets. I know she likes it and can watch the ceremony comfortably." Signor Miccio suggested.

"Great idea," Henrik said." Shall we get them now?"

"When do you want to bring the food down, Henrik, and how will we carry it?" Franco asked.

"On the Viking ship, when we come into the bay. We can load it into the car, bring it to your boatyard, and then sail it to the wedding. Most of it can be warmed up on the BBQ. What do you think?"

"Perfect."

A short while later, they were sitting around the fire pit. John placed another log on the fire.

"What other traditions are customary for a Viking wedding, Henrik?"

"Let me see. Oh yes, I nearly forgot. You'll like this one, John. It is customary for the groom to dig up his ancestor's grave and retrieve the family sword he is buried with. This symbolizes him entering death as a boy and emerging into life as a man."

For a moment, there was silence as John digested this piece of information. He was the only one who knew about the sacred sword being buried with Brother Emmanuel.

"Anyone know who I can dig up and who might have a sword I can use?" Henrik laughed.

John couldn't believe the coincidence. Only a month ago, he was placing the ancient sword into the arms of the monk to protect him on his journey.

"I think, dear boy, the likelihood of you doing that is very remote." Signor Miccio said. "You may have to remain a boy forever."

They laughed, but for John, he had a deep feeling of déjà vu. For a moment, he felt Giovanni had wormed his way into his psyche. Would he ever be able to get him out of his head? In his mind, he could see the body of the beloved monk laid out in his simple coffin, clutching the cross in his arms. He raised his drink and gave a silent prayer to Emmanuel. *'May you rest in peace, my friend.'*

"Before we drink too much, can we just go over the final preparations for tomorrow," Franco said.

"I have bread to make in the morning and the fish to prepare for the BBQ. And, of course, the pig roast, which should take about six hours to cook. Also, we have to transport the food." Henrik suddenly realised there was a lot to do."I'll head back to The Villa and get started."

"Oh no, you don't," Franco said. "This is your last night of freedom. We can't have our Viking warrior going home to cook bread."

"Let the party commence," John shouted as the beer began to flow.

"Certo," (quite right), Signor Miccio agreed.

One beer followed another, and before long, the men were arm in arm, singing loud songs. Henrik was really getting into the spirit of the occasion.

"It is traditional," he said, "for married men to give advice to the young groom to guide him towards a happy marriage."

"Well, it's no good asking me," John laughed. "I would probably say don't do it, but I'm a negative sort of guy besides, Eva is perfect for you."

"Indeed," shouted Franco. "I think you are a match made in heaven. My daughter not only takes after me for her good looks, but she can cook with even the poorest of ingredients and make it superb."

"I agree," Signor Miccio interrupted. "She is also very kind. I would be honoured if she was my daughter."

Franco moved over to hug the elderly man. "Grazie mille. It softens my heart to hear you say that."

"So here is a toast to Eva, my beautiful Viking Princess," Henrik said.

They clinked their bottles and began singing again. This time, a Neapolitan love song.

Wedding Day

(Giorno del Matrimonio)

The morning of the wedding had arrived. Eva's last night as a single girl had been restless. At around 3 a.m, she heard whispering and giggling, and looking out of the window, she could see the men trying to sneak into the house. She assumed they had been on Henrik's 'stag do,' as Signor Miccio was singing quite loudly. It was pure anticipation of the day ahead that was keeping her awake. Smiling, she climbed back into bed and tucked the covers under her chin, giggling with excitement. How lucky she was that Henrik had come into her life. He was kind and funny, and their relationship was easy. They loved the same things and had a passion for food that inspired each other.

Eva had no idea what was going to happen on her wedding day. All she knew was that everything was arranged and she just had to relax and enjoy the surprises as they happened.

The first was when Mary knocked at her door

in the morning. She was carrying an enormous box wrapped in what appeared to be fur. The note inside, written on parchment paper, read:

New Year's Eve - December 31st 2020

Eva,

My princess. You are the love of my life, and I can't wait for you to be my bride.

Please be ready to walk down to the boathouse with your guests to arrive at 4.30 pm and await the arrival of your Viking prince.

Kys kys

Ps: I hope you like your dress

Martha and Samantha came in behind Mary. They each carried similar boxes and were smiling in anticipation of the fun ahead.

"Oh my goodness, of course, it is a Viking wedding. Why didn't I think of that? I'm marrying a Danish man!" Eva cried.

"Are we all ready to see what they have chosen for us?" Sam said. "Come on, Eva, I can't wait to see your dress."

She carefully removed the wrapping and opened the box. Underneath the deep layers of black tissue paper revealed her red dress and matching bouquet of crimson and orange flowers.

"It's beautiful," she stuttered, holding it up for everyone to see, "and look at the fur cloak, oh I love it. I'm going to be a Viking bride."

Each one burst out laughing as they revealed their outfits. Martha was overjoyed with her white floor-length fur coat and strands of deep turquoise jewellery to go with her pale blue dress.

Mary and Samantha each had nordic-designed accessories of heavy metal jewellery, armbands of leather and hair braids, fur cloaks completed the look. John had made for the baby a pure white soft linen dress with a tiny wrist silver bangle and a faux fur wrap. He had also made simple leather boots for everyone, which added authenticity to the outfits.

"Well, they have excelled themselves," Martha smiled. "I think it is absolutely wonderful and I cannot wait for the day to begin."

***

There was a hive of activity as the women prepared the bride for her wedding. Mary and Samantha quickly googled photographs for hair and makeup. Then, the transformation began. Her hair was parted into sections, and the top section was twisted around the nape of her neck in a semi-chignon with the remainder of her dark hair waved and loosely flowing down her back.

Henrik's mother had included a beautiful golden wheat crown, symbolizing fertility and prosperity. The pieces of wheat would be sown into the ground at a future date to continue to fertilize. Tiny red and golden flowers were attached to her hair.

"My dear girl, I think you look absolutely stunning," Martha said.

"Wait until you see the makeup, Martha. Look at this, Eva." Sam passed over a photograph. "Are you up for completing the look?"

"I'm not sure about that," Eva said as she pulled a face. "I mean, look at the eyes. I've never worn heavy smoky makeup like that and the facial paint. I'd look more like a Goth or David Bowie!"

"Umm, OK, let's compromise. How about a small design in red on your forehead? It says on these instructions that red is very symbolic in a Viking wedding. It brings happiness and good luck to the bride."

After much laughing and helped along with a bottle of Prosecco their hair and makeup were finished. Two hours later, everyone was transformed into Nordic royalty.

Eva stood up and raised her glass.

"I'd like to say my undying love goes to you all. You are my family and I love you and want to thank you from the bottom of my heart. I will never forget today and the way you have transformed me into a Viking bride."

Martha moved forward. "Mia cara, of course, we are all family and it is going to be a day to remember. Apparently, John is escorting me down to the cove. He thinks it is too far for me to walk, so he has arranged another mode of transport, which sounds intriguing. So I'll see you all down there."

"Make sure you wrap your fur coat around you, Martha. It's getting a bit cool outside."

"I will, my darling," Martha said as she headed for the door and John who was waiting to take her to the Viking boat.

Half an hour later, the bridal group started the walk down the path towards the cove. They were laughing and singing all the way and the beginnings of a beautiful sunset added to the occasion.

When they reached the cove, they reacted in unison with shouts of delight at the sight, which greeted them. They were escorted to the "altar", and Eva was told her husband to be would join her shortly. She gazed out over the shimmering water, and watched in delight as the sunset and the sky turned the most stunning shade of deep red. In the distance, she could see the 'Viking Ship' sailing into the cove. Henrik stood at the bow, looking every inch a Viking Prince. Tears pricked Eva's eyes with happiness, and everyone around her shouted with excitement.

The ceremony was intimate and romantic, and as the Celebrant tied their hands together to make a knot out of six different coloured ribbons, the tradition was complete and they had become husband and wife. Their kiss sealed their love for each other.

Shouts of joy came from Henrik's parents and family as they watched on the Ipad. As the sunset faded, the flames from the burning logs and candles in the giant holders replaced the light. The guests moved forward to congratulate the happy couple. Very soon, the wedding dinner was in full swing, with the bride and groom at the head of the table.

They started with a delicious fish platter, including traditional herrings with lemon sauce. Fresh green garden salad, hot artichokes with a red pepper dip, and four cheese dips with fresh bread. The main course was a huge beef roast and spit-roasted pork with various sauces. Wooden bowls of roasted potatoes and a medley of vegetables accompanied the meal. Henrik had surpassed himself, but especially with the desserts, which were traditional Danish puddings, including Citronfromage, a lemon mousse topped with cream. He had made tiny pies (aebleskivers), which resembled little puff pancakes with various fillings of pumpkin, chocolate, almond, and fruit berries. At the centrepiece of this delightful banquet stood the Kransekake, the traditional Danish wedding cake. It resembled a tall tower of rings of biscuits in various flavours, including Eva's favourite Amalfi lemons. Henrik held Eva's hand as he escorted her to the table to break the cake (Viking style) with their hands and then invited their guests to do the same. Each guest gave a wedding wish to the happy couple, and Henrik's parents joined in with their own cake.

Mary leaned over to Samantha.

"Wasn't that amazing, Sam? In my wildest dreams, I would never have thought that a group of men could have organised such a wonderful wedding. I mean, look at Henrik and Eva. They are just so in love."

Sam agreed. "It is a perfect way to end such a strange year. Let's hope all this happiness will continue into next year."

The eating and drinking carried on until eventually, people wandered outside to sit by the fire pit under a heaven sent star lit sky. Music was playing, and singing and dancing was an inevitable part of the celebration.

The wedding party stood by the water's edge as the fireworks from Sorrento burst into the night sky to welcome in 2021... a New Year. The magical colours lit up the skyline, and reflections danced on the water, making the moment seem almost spiritual.

Relaxing in the comfort and warmth of her swing seat, Martha enjoyed watching everyone having fun. She wrapped her long fur coat around her and closed her eyes as Signor Miccio began to sing her favourite Neapolitan love song, 'Oh Marie.'

It had been a perfect day. Despite the Covid restrictions Martha felt deeply that love had found a way to create a simple but special occasion and in some ways it was more memorable. Henrik had made a magical memory for everyone to take with them on their life's journey.

She sighed deeply. Her life had been full of journeys but the best ones had been with her husband by her side. They had experienced loss and sadness but she could not deny how fortunate she had been and what a wonderful life they had both enjoyed together. Martha wished with all her heart that George had not died. She could feel his presence sitting by her side. He whispered in her ear.

"Martha, my darling. Isn't this the most beautiful wedding? It reminds me of when we were married. It was such a wonderful moment when you became my wife. You made me the happiest man alive."

Martha answered him in her thoughts.

"I will never forget the time when you had returned to England after spending a week in my father's hotel. I was heartbroken. In that short time I had fallen in love with you and I thought I would never see you again. And then a few weeks later I was walking through Piazza Tasso and there you were. Just standing looking at me." She laughed as she remembered the most important moment in her life. *"And I rushed into your arms and you whispered in my ear... marry me! I can't tell you how wonderful I felt knowing you had come back for me."*

"Oh Martha, you were etched in my heart. When I got back to London I put all my effort into my work, but it wasn't enough. My life was empty... lonely. I needed you and I couldn't face the future without you. Do you remember your father's face when I asked for your hand in marriage? He wasn't pleased was he?"

"Neither was my mother. She wanted me to marry a nice Italian boy and have lots of babies."

"Do you regret not having children, Martha?"

"Oh, George, che sara sara... it wasn't meant to be. My life was perfect. I couldn't have asked for more."

"I'm glad to hear that. It worried me for a long time. Still, we had a good life didn't we?"

"We certainly did and here we are back at my family's villa. It is wonderful to see it again George. When I first came back, in my mind I could hear my mother's voice calling my papa and I saw faces at the windows waving to me. But they are not here now; even my brothers have gone to join my sister and parents."

"Yes, my darling, I have been watching you struggle. You have been so brave to carry on when your heart was broken. And look at what you have done with the place. It looks stunning and I can see all these young people you have surrounded yourself with have been very important to you. By the way, I think you were right to bury the sword with Emmanuel. It was a fitting thing to do."

"Thank you, my love. I knew you would understand. Oh, George, it is so lovely to reminisce together." She laughed. "We had some wonderful holidays, didn't we? I'll never forget Venice. It was somewhere I had always wanted to visit, but sharing it with you was so special. It was truly magical."

"Yes, Venice," George said. "We saw it at the best time before all the tourists took over and spoilt it. Just wandering around the canals in the evenings was quite scary. All those shadows in the dark streets ready to jump out at us."

"You are funny, darling. It was carnival time. Dressing up is part of the drama of it all. Any excuse for a celebration."

"I know, but they do it so well. I wouldn't say I liked the masked look. It was quite frightening!"

"Oh, George, what am I going to do with you?" Martha stopped and stared at her husband. "And what am I going to do without you?" Tears formed in her eyes. "I miss you so much."

"Hush, my love. Today is for romance and memories. Look at that little boat over there. We had such wonderful day trips to Positano and Capri in that vessel, and look at it now, it is a

Viking ship!" They laughed together. "Martha, we were blessed. So many people never have the experiences we have had. To swim in this beautiful cove without a care in the world was really special. Oh, my darling, I love you, but I'm afraid I have to go soon." George said, his voice becoming tender and kind.

"No, George, please don't go. I can't bear it." Martha felt a chill go through her. Her heart physically hurt. She didn't want this moment to end. Fear made her body shiver. "You can't leave me again," she whispered as he held her close. "Tell me, why have you come back now?"

"There is only one reason, Martha, my darling, and that is to take you to a place where we can be together again forever, but only if you are ready."

"You mean you have come back for me again?"

"Yes. There is nothing to be afraid of. Your family is waiting for you."

"Amore mio, I love you deeply, but I'm not ready to die. My life is not finished yet. I have so many plans, and there is a baby to love and look after and George, you know how much I adore you, but I have work to do and ..."

George interrupted her. "Don't worry, my darling, I understand. You have always been a woman on a mission to create a world for others to enjoy. I will be waiting for you when the time is right. I must go now, but I am always by your side until you are ready." He smiled gently.

"Arrivederci amore mio."

Martha and Alfie stared in amazement into George's tranquil face and watched as his translucent figure quietly faded away from this world leaving the two of them behind.

THE END
(LA FINE)

Book One
Ti Amo Sorrento
(I love Sorrento)

Book Two
Tears of Italy
(Lacrime di Italia)

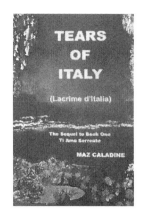

About the Author

Looking back over my life, I often turned to writing to express my thoughts through stories and poems.

Since retiring, after 44 years of secretarial work, I turned a spare bedroom into a study. I indulged my creative juices in drawing, painting, and writing stories. I created and self-published five children's stories. They were set in my favourite seaside town of Robin Hood's Bay in North Yorkshire and featured the crazy seagulls that live there.

My biggest passion in life has always been

anything Italian. When I was 18, I worked in hotels in Sorrento for four years. I have always remembered this fantastic experience, working in busy kitchens and getting to know and love Italian people.

When my holiday was cancelled in 2020 because of Coronavirus, I started writing my first romantic/dramatic novel, Ti Amo Sorrento, set in an old Italian villa. My audience was aimed at tourists who felt like me and were missing Italy's beauty, sunshine, and excitement because of cancelled holidays. I hope I have managed to bring romance and love into the world of my readers.

After I had finished my first book, my readers asked me what happened next. Well, I was wondering that myself, so I decided to let my characters tell their story. I now know, and it is a pleasure to pass this on to you in the form of Book Two, Tears of Italy (Lacrime d'Italia).

I have loved this whole experience of escaping into a world of Italian nostalgia. It is the second best thing to living there.

I am now 73 and have experienced all the ups and downs that life throws at you. I was born in the UK and grew up in the 1950s. I fell in love and lived in Italy in the swinging sixties. I emigrated to Canada on my own in the 1980s and returned home a year later with my 6-week-old daughter. Through the decades, I have seen a lot of changes. I have learnt how to stand on my own two feet and survive, and I hope this adds to my writing inspiration, creativity, and love of life.

I am now happily married and live in a Derbyshire stone cottage in the pretty town of Matlock with beautiful views of the valley and stunning sunsets.

Maz Caladine